Let's Be Friends…*Again*

Sydney Reneé

Let's Be Friends…*Again*

For more information, please visit:
www.thediaryof-she.com.

ISBN: 979-8-9859044-8-2

Let's Be Friends...Again

Chapter One
Ashley

"...how long did you know?"

"Know what?" Ashley asked as she sat on the edge of Nasir's bed.

"About Rebecca...how long did you know?"

Hesitant to answer, Ashley kept her eyes glued to the floor.

Maybe, he won't press the issue, she thought, but that theory quickly went out the window when Nasir walked over to her side of the bed, throwing her phone at her.

"Wow is this is how it's going to be?" she asked, picking her phone up, surprised at the amount of aggression he possessed. It was scary, especially since she was carrying his baby.

"I know you heard me, Ashley."

"First of all, back the fuck up. You're making me uncomfortable right now."

"Talk!"

"...it's been two years."

"So, was this some kind of sick game to get me to be with you?" Nasir's asked.

1

Ashley could see him getting madder with each word rolling off his tongue. It was the last thing she wanted to deal with and the alcohol he consumed wasn't helping. Nasir was drinking more than usual, but Ashley did her best not to make a big deal of it.

"It's nothing like that...I promise." She stood up, trying to calm him down.

As much as she wanted Nasir, she didn't want him to think that she had some master plan to break up his relationship. If that was truly the case, she would have contacted him years ago.

"Well, what is it like, Ashley? Please, explain it to me, because I'm starting to feel like I lost the woman I love because you had a hidden agenda."

Nasir didn't mean for it to slip that he was still in love with Rebecca, but he was, and it was hard for him to let go. This situation showed him it was possible to be in love with two women at the same time, but Ashley was the one carrying his child.

"...and there it is," she said, throwing her hands in the air. "She's who you really want to be with, but I didn't force you to do a damn thing that night. I didn't put a gun to your head and tell you to fuck me. You could have walked away like you did when we were in college, but you made a choice."

Ashley began pacing back and forth, giving Nasir the same energy, the energy he had been giving her for months.

"Sure, I knew about her when I ran into you, but I gave you an opportunity to tell me that there was a woman in your life…didn't I?" She paused, waiting for Nasir to answer, but instead, he just stood there silent. "But clearly you didn't care enough to open your fucking mouth."

"That's not the point, Ashley," he said, turning around to face her. "You're pregnant with my child, and you were going to take that information to the grave."

"You're damn right I was," she snapped. "Seeing as though she's with Brandon, what reason was there to tell you? It wouldn't have changed what took place. If I really wanted to break you and Rebecca up, I would have years ago. When I went searching for you on Facebook, I saw that you were living in L.A. and in a relationship, so I kept my distance. The night Shantel ran into you guys, she told her sister that you and I used to be a thing, and I thought it was fate," she said, moving closer to Nasir, hoping her touch would calm him.

"Honestly, I don't want to hear what you have to say…it's bullshit," Nasir said before he walked into the bathroom.

Feeling uncomfortable, Ashley grabbed her things and was gone before Nasir could notice.

Chapter Two
Ashley

Four-Months Later...

Sitting in her new four-bedroom home in the Hollywood Hills, Ashley was everything but happy. There she was about to enter her 8th month of pregnancy, and she and Nasir still weren't on the best of terms. The trip she wanted to go on was canceled before it was even booked. The moment Nasir found out that she knew about Rebecca, he was livid. No matter how much she tried to convince him that it wasn't her intent to break them up, he wasn't ready to accept it...not yet.

Ashley was surprised he hadn't called their relationship quits, but she thought it was partly because he had always wanted a family and she didn't blame him. He had two loving parents who had been going strong for over forty years, and that's exactly what he wanted for himself. No matter what Nasir and Ashley were going through, he would do his best to make sure that they worked out.

"What's wrong?" he asked, walking into the nursery.

They both had plans to make this home their forever home, so he picked the second largest room for their baby boy to grow in. The entire room was white with sprinkles of navy and brown on the furniture. Ashley was sitting in her rocking chair looking at one of the baby books with a sad face.

"Talking to me today?" she asked, sarcastically.

"Let's not do that," he said, kneeling to rub her stomach.

"Are we good, Nasir?"

"I'm here, aren't I?"

"...*physically*, but you've been distant. I'm getting closer to having this baby, and I still feel like you're not sure about us," she said, touching her stomach.

"We've had a small setback, but I promise everything is going to be fine before our son gets here." Looking at her stomach, he said, "Daddy can't wait to meet you," before he kissed it.

The moment his lips touched her skin, their child began to do backflips.

"Looks like he can't wait to meet you either," Ashley smiled. It was just what she needed—a sign that everything was going to be okay.

Getting up off the floor, Nasir planted a kiss on her forehead.

"Is that the only thing bothering you, Ash?"

Can he read my mind right now? Damn, she thought, as she continued to rock in the chair and stare out the window

"Yeah, that's all," she lied.

"Okay, well, I'm going to head out for the day. I'm showing a house to one of my old clients, and I don't want to be late."

"All right. I love you, Nasir. I'll let you know how the rest of this baby shower planning goes," she said, struggling out of the rocking chair.

"Don't forget to get the final guest list from your mother. I want to make sure we have enough space at the venue for everyone."

"I'll send it over to you today," he said, giving her a kiss and hug.

Trying to get her mind off what was indeed bothering her, Ashley walked over to the closet and began removing baby clothes from the hangers. It was only 9 in the morning on a Saturday, but she didn't have to meet with the planner until 3.

Brittany was going to meet her at the venue to help with some last-minute changes to the decor and taste some of the treats she planned to have set up at the sweets table.

Throughout her pregnancy, all Ashley craved was sugar. When she took her glucose test, she was terrified that they were going to tell her she had diabetes.

As Ashley pulled the clothes off the hangers, she began separating them by color, so she could wash and put them away. The baby shower wasn't for another two weeks, but they already had a ton of clothes. Nasir's mother had been sending clothes every other week since she found out she was going to be a G-Ma.

All the joy her unborn son brought made Ashley wish that her mother was still around to witness the mother she would be, but then again...they might have been better off without her.

It was going on 12 p.m., and Ashley had finished washing all the clothes in the closet. All she needed to do was wash the towels, burp cloths, socks, and blankets she had tucked away in his drawers.

Too bad, I'll be doing this again in a few weeks, she thought, as she walked out the room.

Ashley entered the white master bedroom she and Nasir shared. She was against the all-white theme for the longest because she didn't want to worry about spilling anything on the furniture. She and Nasir made a deal that if most of the color in the house was white, she could have her share of neutral colors if it matched their maple hardwood floors. When it came to the house, she left most of the decisions up to Nasir since he was the one paying for it, and, of course, he chose a modern home because he loved living, in what looked like, a glass house. She just hoped no one came around to throw stones.

Brit:

Still need me to come with you to meet the planner?

Getting out of the shower, Ashley saw that she had a message from Brittany. Even though they were supposed to meet up, she knew whenever Brittany asked if she was needed for something, it meant she made other plans.

As much as Ashley wanted to go off on her for trying to ditch her last minute, she didn't because she honestly didn't need Brittany's help; she just wanted someone to keep her company.

Ashley:
I was hoping you could come for support...but no biggie. I'll see if Nicole or Regina can swing by.

Brit:
I'm sorry, Ash. I forgot I was going to take my siblings to Universal Studios today since they've never been.

Ashley:
Don't worry about it. Just make sure you don't miss my baby shower. Love you!

Brit:
Love you too!

Ashley didn't want to bother Regina or Nicole; both had been caught up in their own relationships. Regina and Gary were still going strong to Ashley's surprise, and Nicole...well, she was in the midst of planning a wedding. Ashley still couldn't believe her sister was getting married after only knowing this man for six months. She tried

8

to talk Nicole out of going forward with the wedding, but Nicole was adamant about walking down the aisle as soon as Ashley healed from childbirth. Ashley agreed to back off Nicole, but something about Derek was off, and every time her brother Nick saw him, he looked like he wanted to take his head off. He and Nicole got into an argument about it, and, of course, it turned to Nick saying fuck the wedding.

Ashley was so over their bickering, but he was right...*fuck that shit!*

Chapter Three
Nasir

Pulling into the driveway of the five-bedroom, six-bath house in Beverly Hills he was about to show, Nasir found himself jealous, wishing he had purchased the home for himself, but it was too big for his family. Nasir was still trying to figure out how his client was able to afford to look at a home of this caliber, but he wasn't going to ask any questions.

Unlocking the door, he noticed a car pull up.

"It's been quite some time," a woman said, as she got out and walked up to Nasir.

"Nice to see you again, Diane. I know it's been a while, but from the looks of things, I think it's safe to say that you're doing great."

"I'd say I'm doing pretty damn good," she smiled. "Now, are you going to show me this beauty, or what?"

"After you," Nasir motioned Diane into the house.

Before walking completely in, Diane was already in awe. She twirled in a circle, admiring the architecture of the home, which had panoramic windows that offered incredible views of the hills. Diane could see herself sitting outside by one of the two pools the

10

home provided, sipping on wine as the love of her life fed her chocolate-covered strawberries. Never in her life had she imagined she would live in such luxury, but she was just a few steps away.

"I see you already like what the house has to offer," Nasir smiled, as he showed Diane around.

Not only were there two pools, but the backyard also had a tennis court. Inside, there was a movie theater and a full bar that needed to be stocked, of course. Like Nasir's home, the color scheme was mostly white throughout with some black and neutral colors spread around. The floor was a beautiful stone, but Diane's favorite part of the house was the walk-in closet. It was like walking into an upscale boutique. She also didn't have to worry about any of Derek's things crowding her space, because there were two master bedroom-sized closets.

"When was this house built?" she asked, as she followed Nasir into the kitchen where he had a few appetizers and a bottle of champagne sitting on the marble island.

"It was built in 1934, and the last time it was remodeled was in 1967."

"You're kidding me. It looks so new."

"Well, everything inside, as far as the furnishings go, is new, but besides that, this house hasn't been remodeled since." Popping the bottle, he poured the bubbling champagne into two flutes. "Do you have somewhere to go?" Nasir asked as he handed her the glass.

"Not until later." Diane took a sip. "And especially not before I put an offer down on the house. I must have it."

"Today?" he asked, surprised.

"Yes, I can write you the check right now…unless you don't want to get this commission," she said, reaching for her purse as if she was about to leave.

"Nope, I need that," he laughed. "I have a family I have to take care of now."

"A family?"

Diane was being nosy per usual. She knew he and Rebecca were no longer an item, but she just didn't know why.

"Yeah, I have a baby boy on the way with my girlfriend," he responded, knowing he fucked up.

Rebecca and Brandon were unaware that Nasir was on his way to becoming a dad, and he made sure that Regina and Gary promised not to say a word. Now that he told Diane, he knew by Monday morning, Rebecca would be in the baby loop.

Nasir didn't know why he was trying to protect Rebecca's feelings, but he felt it was something he had to do, and it annoyed the hell out of Ashley. She barely used social media, but she couldn't even post pictures from her maternity shoot, which caused their biggest argument to date.

"*Awww*, congrats, Nas. I know you are going to be a great dad…I can't wait to have a child of my own," she sighed.

"Thank you. I'm sure you'll have some kids running around this huge place sooner than you think."

"I sure hope so," she said, pulling out her checkbook. "Before I write this check…is it okay if it's coming from my boyfriend's account? He signed it already. I just need to write out the amount."

"No problem. Can you do me a favor and just call him for me, so I can verify? Also, I can't officially call this house 'yours' until the offer is accepted, and we get all the paperwork done."

"That's not a problem," she said, pulling out her phone. "I trust you'll return my check if this doesn't fall through…hey, babe, can you let the realtor know it's okay for me to use your account for this house while we wait for our paperwork to go through? I have you on speaker."

"…hey, if she wants the house, it's good to go. Thanks for checking in…I need to get back to work but love you. I'll call you later."

Damn, that voice sounds familiar, Nasir thought to himself.

"Well, it looks like you're good to go, Diane. I'll get all the necessary paperwork to you. Make sure you get it to me by Monday. I'll do my best to get your offer accepted. You're the only person who's come around with money in hand."

"I can't wait." She jumped up and gave Nasir a hug.

Nasir walked Diane to the door and went back in to clean up the kitchen before locking up. Once he got to his car, he finally looked at the check Diane gave him, only to see Derek's name scribbled on the front.

"How the fuck am I going to tell Ashley this?" he said, shaking his head.

Chapter Four

Rebecca

Brandon and Rebecca's relationship was going better than they could have envisioned. Rebecca rented out her apartment and moved in with Brandon shortly after they became official. They were inseparable and only felt it was the next move.

Rebecca was still going strong when it came to her blog and the podcast with Nikki, so Brandon went out of his way to surprise her with a studio to record in.

Getting out of bed, Rebecca saw a path of white rose petals leading out of the room. Wondering what was going on, she yelled out Brandon's name but received no response.

"Babe," she continued to call out as she made her way down the steps.

At the dining room table, where the rose petals stopped, there was a bouquet of her favorite flowers with a note attached, along with breakfast

"*Awww*, he made me breakfast," she smiled, as she picked up a piece of bacon and stuffed it into her mouth. *Mmmm. Crispy just like I like it.*

15

Picking up the note Brandon left, Rebecca began to read it aloud:

Good morning, angel face! I had to get to set earlier than expected and didn't want to wake you. I hope you love your flowers and enjoy the breakfast I made. I may be home late, but if you aren't busy, come check out the set today. Love you, and I'll check in later.

"How did I get so lucky?" she asked herself, as she sat down to enjoy her breakfast alone.

Nikki Shay was coming over so they could work on their book, which Rebecca was having some trouble with. For the most part, she knew Nikki's writing style, but she was struggling to match it and come up with ideas for her characters, which is why she desperately needed her to come over.

Nikki was comfortable using her personal experiences, but Rebecca seemed to have a hard time. As easy as it was to put her relationship out there on her YouTube channel, it was hard to put it into words and still make it sound juicy rather than depressing. She also didn't want any of her exes coming out of the grave they were buried in, complaining about her putting her real life into her fictitious characters.

Finishing up the last of the eggs on her plate, Rebecca got up, placed her dishes in the dishwasher with last night's dirty dishes, and pressed the *start* button. Walking back upstairs into the master bedroom, she grabbed her phone from off the dresser and texted Brandon.

Rebecca:
Good morning, handsome. Thank you for the breakfast. It was delicious.

Within a minute, Brandon texted back.

Brandon:
You deserve everything you get...what are you doing?

Rebecca:
Don't make me blush, babe. But I'm about to take a bubble bath before Nikki comes over.

Brandon:
Now, you know it's my job to keep that smile coming.

Brandon:
But, babe, I need to get back to directing this scene. Love you, enjoy your lavender bubble bath, because I know that's what it is lol...oh, and send me something sexy.

Rebecca:
Oh, gosh...love you too.

"Alexa, play Summer Walker," Rebecca requested, as she removed her silk robe and slipped off her boy shorts.

Stepping into the bath, she eased her way down into the water and laid her head back. *This is exactly what I needed.* Just as she was getting relaxed, her phone went off. Reaching over to check, it was Brandon asking for his special surprise.

I'ma fuck around and break my shit, she thought, as she grabbed her phone to send him a quick video of her playing in the bubbles. He would appreciate what she had for him when he returned home more than a video that he might not be able to look at until a few hours from now.

*****

"You're thinking way too hard," Nikki said, as she looked at Rebecca, whose head was about to explode.

"Imagine that you're sitting in front of your camera, recording a vlog for your audience. Let it flow."

"I'm not an author like you, Nikki; it's different," Rebecca said, frustrated.

"Okay, then…let's try this," Nikki said, pulling out her laptop. "Tell me about the time you caught your fiancé cheating."

"Do I have to, Nikki?"

"No, you don't *have* to, but I promise you, it'll spark something great. A lot of exceptional stories come from pain," she tried to reassure Rebecca. "And remember, this is fiction, so we can exaggerate as much as we want, and you can make the outcome be whatever you want."

"Shall I start from the beginning?" Rebecca asked.

"Start wherever you'd like. This is your story."

Taking a deep breath, Rebecca began to talk about her relationship with her ex-fiancé—Elliot Jones.

"I should have seen it coming after I had my miscarriage...something in him changed," she said, shedding a tear.

Shit is about to get real, Nikki thought, as she typed away.

Chapter Five
Brandon & Gary

Today was the big day; Brandon and Gary were starting production on their film—*When Kings Rise*. Their investors gave them all the money they needed to hire who they wanted, book locations needed, and do everything else that came along with making a film.

The film was based on parts of their lives, and they didn't want anyone coming in to change their story.

"You ready to shoot this scene?" Gary asked, placing his hand on Brandon's shoulder.

"Yep. Are you?"

"No, but that's why we're getting this shit out the way now, and hopefully, we won't have to reshoot it."

Today, they were shooting the toughest and most emotional scene in the movie—their father's death. For the longest, they believed he was killed in a drive-by on some *wrong place, wrong time* shit, but when they started writing their script, they went to their mother for some backstory. It was then that she finally told them the truth. Details of what happened affected Gary more than

Brandon. Hearing what his mother had to endure had Brandon wondering how she continued raising them alone. She never re-married, but she managed to raise two strong, successful, black men; never once having to worry about them running to the streets looking for a father figure.

Although everything they were shooting was fake, Gary had to walk away in the middle of the scene; it felt too real for him.

Monica was playing their mother and as nervous as Brandon was, she was already proving to him they made the right decision. She cried on demand, and the scene depicting a horrible sexual assault almost brought Brandon to tears, as he sat back and imagined what happened in his family's home.

The night their father died two men came looking for him. They beat and assaulted their mother, and then tied her to a chair while they waited for their dad to come home. Once he arrived, they made their mother watch as they tortured and killed him.

"My god," Brandon said, giving Monica a hug, "Rebecca would be so proud of you...I wish she could have come to set."

"Thank you, but I'm glad she didn't. This was tough for me, and the more retakes we did the more I felt like it happened to me," she said, looking up at Brandon. "Rebecca being here would've *just* made it harder...where is Gary by the way?" She

21

noticed him walking away in the middle of filming.

"He needed to take a breather. I was about to go check on him now. I'll be back soon to shoot a few more scenes," he said, walking to the back.

As he walked into the office, he saw Gary sitting on the couch with a drink in hand, staring off into the distance.

"You good?" Brandon asked, pouring himself a drink, and then sitting down next to Gary.

"How could mom hide this from us for so long?" he responded, throwing back his Hennessy. "What if we had been there that night? Even worse…what if they killed her?" Gary was finally letting all his emotions out.

Brandon knew it bothered him hearing how their dad had robbed some big-time drug dealers, and his mother was left to deal with the consequences. She had always painted this beautiful picture of their father, always leaving out who he really was. Gary didn't want his mother to see how it hurt him, but he was breaking down inside.

"Stop worrying about the *what-ifs*. Mom is here, and we're here, thriving, and happy. Dad would be proud of all we've become." Brandon tried to comfort his brother.

"But he's supposed to be here too, B. I've finally met a woman I'm ready to settle down with. We're living out our dreams, and he's not here to see any of it," Gary said, wiping away the tear that was rolling down his face.

"I know, man, but you can't think of it like that. We have to keep living and remembering the good times."

"You right," Gary said, getting up to give his brother a hug. "Let's get back to work."

"...I'll be right there," Brandon said, looking down at his phone.

"Wifey?" Gary laughed.

"Man, get out of here."

Opening his messages, he saw a video from Rebecca.

She really sent me something, he smiled, thinking she was going to make him wait till he got back home. Rebecca always acted shy when it was time to take off her clothes, but Brandon didn't understand why.

Clicking on the video, he got hard as he watched Rebecca rub bubbles across her breasts.

I cannot wait to get back, he thought to himself, before walking back out to the set.

"*Action!*" he heard Gary yell, as he closed the door behind him.

Chapter Six
Ashley & Regina

"Why didn't you call me earlier?"

"I don't know. I just assumed you were busy with your man," Ashley replied.

She was about ten minutes late getting to her meeting with the planner and was going to be charged a late fee. If not for Regina putting on her best "Karen" performance, Ashley would've spent an extra $100 for nothing because the meeting didn't take but 30 minutes.

A few hours before leaving the house, Ashley began to feel weak and was afraid to drive, but she refused to cancel. The baby shower was in exactly two weeks, and she wanted the final touches locked in. Before calling Regina, she called Nicole, but she had a class to teach. Thank goodness Regina was able to rush over.

"Starting today, I have all the time in the world, so whatever you need, I'm here," Regina said, as she followed behind Ashley.

"You and Gary break up or something?"

"Girl No! That man loves me," Regina blushed. "He and Brandon started filming, so he'll be gone for most of the day."

"Oh, okay," Ashley responded, slightly disappointed. She knew the closer they got to each other, the closer she was to encountering Rebecca again.

"Why would you even think that?"

"Because you two have literally been inseparable. I still can't believe you got that dog to behave."

"That part," Regina agreed. "But this break is needed. It'll give us some time to miss each other."

Ashley knew exactly what she meant. Normally, the job was Ashley's break from Nasir, but since getting a home together, he was all she saw in the morning and at night. Once upon a time, it would've been a dream to come home to him every day, but since they'd been having problems, she prayed for time apart. The only thing that worried her about time apart was their realizing they weren't meant for each other.

"I feel you on that," she snapped her fingers in agreeance. "Nasir's ass been having this little fake attitude with me ever since he saw that text you sent me."

"Please, don't tell me he's still tripping off that," Regina said, rolling her eyes.

"He swears he's over it, but now and then, I'll catch him stalking her and Brandon's page. I know he still loves her, but *fuck*…at least, try to focus on the family *we're* creating."

Thinking about the whole situation was starting to piss her off. Maybe, it was time for them to end up in a room together, so he could see that he and Rebecca were over for good. Then, maybe, he would concentrate on making things work with her, with no distractions.

"Yeah, he needs to let it go. It's not your fault they broke up. You might have known he had a woman, but he knew too," Regina said, shaking her head. "Plus, I'm kind of glad that Shantel's sneaky-ass sent that shit."

"Why?

"I don't know what Nas' relationship was like with Rebecca, but watching her and Brandon, they both seem genuinely happy. He wants to propose," Regina said, looking over at Ashley.

"Stop lying?" Maybe, I'll invite them to the baby shower now," Ashley snickered.

"Well, since you thinking that can me and Gary tell they ass you pregnant? You know I hate secrets, and I've been holding this one in *for*ever."

"Go for it!"

Chapter Seven
Monica & Nikki

It was almost midnight, and Monica wanted nothing more than to relax with her woman. Nikki invited her over for dinner and a movie, but all she wanted was a nice hot bath and to rest her head on the woman she loved. Monica had involved herself with women for fun in the past, but nothing was ever as serious as her relationship with Nikki; Together they had a future.

Pulling up to Nikki's gate, Monica put in the code to get into the complex, pulled into Nikki's guest parking stall, and put the guest placard on the windshield before she got out. The management in that complex was strict, and she refused to wake up in the morning to a missing car.

Nikki must've heard Monica walk up the stairs because she opened the door just as she was about to knock.

"I missed you," she said, kissing Monica.

"I missed you too," Monica responded, as she followed Nikki into the living room. "Today was a long day."

"Well, it's your lucky night, because I already ran you a hot bath."

This woman is incredible, Monica thought, as Nikki led her into the master bedroom. No man had ever catered to her as Nikki had. Sure, they would shower her with gifts, but they also did what they wanted to her. They treated her like an object, but with Nikki, it was different.

Walking into the room, Monica could smell vanilla candles. Before Monica could turn around to thank Nikki, she heard "Angel of Mine" by Monica pop on.

"Look at you... being romantic," Monica said, turning around to kiss Nikki. "Are you joining me?"

"I try...but, no, this is all for you. I'll watch," she laughed, as she began to undress Monica.

"I got it..."

"Hush and let me cater to you," Nikki interrupted.

Nikki washed Monica from head to toe, not missing a spot. She was so relaxed that she began drifting to sleep until she felt Nikki's hands exploring her body.

"I knew that would wake you," she giggled.

"I thought we were going to watch a movie?" Monica asked softly, as Nikki continued to massage her clit.

"Wouldn't you rather me please you?"

Standing, Nikki began to undress until she stood fully naked in front of Monica. Walking towards the glass double-head shower, she turned the water on and stepped in. Watching Monica watch her, she started to dance seductively and motioned for Monica to join her.

"You're the most beautiful woman I've ever seen," Monica said, stepping into the shower.

Pulling Nikki close, Monica began kissing her as the water rained down on them. Massaging between her legs, she kissed Nikki's neck, making her way down to Nikki's pussy where she placed small kisses on her lower lips.

"Wait...," Nikki moaned, as Monica licked and sucked on her clit.

Ignoring her, Monica continued to make love to Nikki with her tongue.

"Babe," Nikki let out a sigh of relief, "I wanted to be the one to please you."

"Well, let's take this to the bed," Monica said, grabbing Nikki's hand. Monica was never one for giving, but she was extremely comfortable with Nikki. Hearing her moan made her juices flow.

Laying Nikki across the bed, Monica began kissing her passionately, while they massaged each other's flowers. They quickly found themselves in a 69 position, trying to see who would cum first. It was a game they liked to play.

Just as Nikki was about to cum, she felt Monica's mouth stop moving, and a moan released along with her sweet nectar. Nikki proceeded to grind her pussy against

Monica's face as she continued to lick and suck up Monica's juices.

The two of them pleased each other for hours until they finally passed out in each other's arms. It was a night they both needed.

Chapter Eight
Rebecca & Brandon

Sitting in Brandon's home theater, Rebecca snacked on popcorn and Milk Duds while watching *A Thin Line Between Love & Hate*. Brandon had all the classics in his movie collection, which Rebecca loved, especially since she enjoyed spending her free time on the couch watching movies all day. Every Sunday, they would lounge around in their pajamas, order takeout, and watch movies.

Brandon assured her that although he'd be gone most of the week, Sunday was still their day. It didn't bother her much since she worked all week too and could take her time with her other projects.

After finally spilling her heart out to Nikki about her relationship with her ex-fiancé, Rebecca cried until she had no more tears left. Besides Monica, Rebecca never talked about him to anyone. For so long, she tried to give him a baby, but she failed. It made her feel worthless, and he reminded her of how broken she was every chance he got. And, seeing as though she and Nasir had also slipped up a few times and never got pregnant, it had her wondering if she'd ever be able to have kids.

"Babe," Brandon called out, as he walked into the theater.

Rebecca had passed out during the movie while waiting for him to get home. He took longer than he said he would because he got caught up with Gary.

"Aye, babe," he called out again, as he turned off the projector, but Rebecca was dead to the world.

Picking her up, Brandon walked towards the elevator that led up to his room and placed her down on the bed. He had been gone all day and refused to hop in bed dirty as hell, so he went to take a shower, but not before kissing Rebecca on the forehead; she looked like an angel when she was asleep.

Man, I love that girl, he thought, as he walked away.

"…I love you."

"Huh?" Brandon responded in shock, thinking Rebecca was asleep.

"I said, 'I love you,' Brandon," she repeated herself, as she sat up, rubbing her eyes.

"My bad…I heard you, babe. It's just that I thought you were sleeping."

"I was, but I felt your kiss and smelled your cologne…come get in bed; it's late."

"I will as soon as I take this shower."

"Fine," Rebecca whined, making Brandon shake his head and laugh as he walked away.

Forty minutes later, Brandon was feeling like a new man, ready to lie next to his dream woman...who was sound asleep once again.

Climbing into bed, he wrapped his arms around Rebecca and held her close, kissing her on the neck before closing his eyes. Rebecca turned her body around and kissed Brandon softly on the lips.

"I missed you," she said, still half asleep.

"I always miss you."

Brandon opened his eyes and began to kiss Rebecca passionately. Lifting her gown, he grabbed her ass, pulling her closer, and to his surprise, she didn't have any panties on.

Rebecca could feel him rising, but she was too tired for four-play. Rolling on top of him, she grabbed his dick and then slid down on it.

"Damn, babe, you were waiting on me, weren't you?"

Rebecca was dripping wet, and Brandon loved how smoothly he was able to slide deep inside of her. He swore her love below was made just for him.

"Yes, daddy," she moaned, as she grinded on him slowly.

Pulling her gown over her head, Brandon massaged her breasts, as she continued to bounce up and down on his dick.

"You want daddy to make you cum?" he groaned, as Rebecca placed her hands on the headboard, starting to pick up speed.

"Yes, daddy. Make me cum all over that dick."

Brandon loved when Rebecca talked to him dirty. She was always so sweet, but in the bedroom, she turned into the biggest freak he had ever come across.

Taking charge, Brandon flipped her on her back, placed her legs on his shoulders, and began fucking the life out of her.

"I'm about to cum," she screamed as Brandon thrust himself deeper into her stomach, stroking until he came and collapsing onto her chest.

"I'm sorry, babe," he sighed, as he rolled over.

"For what?"

"Letting my kids off in you." He began rubbing her belly.

"Don't be." She kissed him before she rolled out the bed to go to the bathroom.

I probably can't have babies anyway.

Chapter Nine
Nicole

"What the fuck, Derek?"

"Man, please, don't start that shit today," he said, walking into the house as if there was nothing wrong.

Nicole had been calling and texting his phone all weekend, but it kept going to voicemail. Now, there he was, strolling into the house past dinnertime. For months, he had become extremely distant, but Nicole wanted to give him the benefit of the doubt. At first, his excuse was he had a huge caseload that he needed to get through, and it was all believable. Derek worked his ass off and hardly lost any cases, but Nicole had adapted to his schedule. She knew that on weekends he would go to work for a couple of hours on Saturday, and for the rest of the weekend, he had people who handled any additional work that needed to be taken care of.

"Where in the fuck were you?" she yelled, as he brushed past her, going right into their bedroom.

"Calm down, Nicole. I'm not about to do this shit with your young ass tonight."

"You not, but I am."

35

Nicole was on his heels, following him directly into the bathroom. She was supposed to be marrying this man in just four months, but it seemed like the minute he met Ashley, he started acting different. She was tired of his lies, and if he had underlying feelings about their relationship, he needed to say it. Nicole was prepared to work through whatever the matter was, but now, she was trying to force the truth out of him. Still ignoring her, Derek turned on the shower and proceeded to get undressed.

"I know you hear me, Derek," she yelled, reaching over to turn the shower off. "Where the fuck were you all damn weekend?"

"You better move, Nic," he responded aggressively.

"...or what? Are you going to chastise me like some little-ass kid? We both know you love to do that."

"Man, get the fuck out my way, Nicole," he said, shaking his head.

"Answer my question," she demanded before slapping him.

Without thinking, he backhanded her and watched as she dropped to the floor. They would have intense arguments here and there, but Nicole never thought this day would come.

"I hate you," she screamed, as she picked herself up, rushing to the closet to pack a bag. "I'm leaving."

"Bye," he said, turning the shower back on.

"Really? You're just going to *let* me leave?" she asked, walking back into the bathroom.

"If that's what you want to do, I'm not going to stop you."

"Wow," she said, walking out of the bathroom again.

Nicole knew she wasn't about to leave; she had nowhere to go, but she, at least, wanted Derek to feel guilty for what he did. She could have gone and stayed with the guestroom at Ashley's house, but she didn't want to get into why she left her home in the first place. Plus, Nicole could already feel the side of her face swelling.

The other person she usually called on, she couldn't. Nick hadn't talked to her in months and was too busy playing stepdad to some woman's child. Nicole didn't approve of his relationship or him taking on the responsibility of someone else's child, but she had to admit the new life he was living was keeping him out of trouble.

Putting her bag back into the closet, she made her way to the kitchen to make herself a drink and get some ice for her face.

Thank God, I don't have to go to work tomorrow, she thought, as she held the ice towel against her cheek, hoping it wouldn't look too bad when she woke up. *I can't believe he hit me.*

As she took a sip of her drink, she thought back to the times she watched her mom get beat on. Nicole swore she'd never let that happen in her relationship, but tonight showed her that anything was possible.

"I'm sorry, baby girl," Derek said, rubbing her shoulders.

"Sure, you are."

Nicole was still in disbelief, and that little hour he had spent in the shower wasn't going to make her forget shit.

"I'm serious. You know I love you." Derek leaned down to kiss her cheek. "After work Saturday, I got a call that my mom fell and sprained her ankle, so I ended up staying with her for the weekend," he lied.

"You could have at least called me and said that. I would have understood. Instead, you had me worrying like crazy. It doesn't help that you've already been distant from me. On top of that," she turned around to look at him, "you barely touch me these days."

They went from having sex almost every day to a few days out of the month.

"Babe, I've been really busy, but I'm going to fix it…starting right now."

Swooping Nicole up and placing her down on the couch, Derek spread her legs and began to explore her peach with his tongue. She tried to push him away but couldn't resist the feeling of pleasure.

Chapter Ten
Ashley & Nasir

A week later...

"You want to come with me to show a few houses to-day?" Nasir asked.

"I don't think I have the energy. I'm too tired and getting entirely too big to be walking around houses and sitting in a car all day," Ashley said, placing her hand on top of her belly.

Since she was getting closer and closer to her due date, she decided to take off a few months early. Nasir could tell that she was getting bored, but the back and forth was becoming too much for her body to handle.

"You sure? I know you can't stand being in the house all day."

"I'm positive," she said, rolling out the bed to go to the bathroom. Her bladder was about to explode at any minute.

"Well, I'm going to make you some breakfast before I get ready for my day."

Nasir got out the bed too and headed to the kitchen to make himself a smoothie and get Ashley all fueled up for her day. He'd usually wake up early to get in his morning run, but, today, he wanted to lay in bed for

39

a while. Plus, he was still trying to figure out if he should tell Ashley about Nicole's fiancé putting a down payment on a house that cost $1.5 million.

Nicole was practically his little sister, and if they found out he knew about Derek being unfaithful, they'd probably never forgive him for keeping it a secret.

Just as Nasir was about to go deeper into his thoughts, his phone began to ring. It was the owners of the mansion Diane put an of-fer in for.

"Good morning, Nasir."

"Good morning, Mrs. Wilson. How are you this morning?"

"I'm doing lovely. Just wanted to call to let you know that we are accepting the offer and will be out of the house in about a week," she said, eagerly.

"Thank you for letting me know. I will let Diane know that she can start packing up and be in by, let's say…next Monday?"

"Sounds good! Have a great day, Nasir."

"You too, Mrs. Wilson."

"…Diane? Isn't that Rebecca's boss? What do you have to tell her?" Ashley asked, standing by the dining room table with her arms folded.

"Oh, just that she can move into her new home by next week."

"When did you take her to look at a house?"

"What are all the questions about?" Nasir asked as he placed her bacon, eggs, and toast on a plate.

"Oh, nothing," she said, sarcastically.

Grabbing her plate from the kitchen island, she walked over to the table and sat down.

"I just didn't know that you were keeping close ties with Rebecca's people like that."

Here we go.

"If you'd like to know, I knew her *before* I knew who Rebecca was. Secondly, instead of worrying about who my clients are, all of which help us live the way we do, maybe, you should be asking your sister about that shady-ass nigga she's about to marry."

"What's that supposed to mean?" Ashley questioned, irritated as hell.

"Nothing," Nasir said, grabbing his smoothie and walking towards their bedroom. "I need to get ready for work."

As much as Ashley wanted to ignore what just came out of his mouth, all she could think about was Nasir knowing something that he didn't want anyone else to know, but if it involved her sister, he needed to let it the fuck out.

Chapter Eleven
Rebecca

Rebecca sat behind her desk, which was now in her own office with her name plastered across the door, like a real boss. Diane was finally giving her the credit she deserved for helping her build up the company, and Rebecca was enjoying every bit of it.

She wasn't sure if Diane decided that it was time to start being more positive and empowering, or if the dick she was getting had her in a good mood, but whatever it was, Rebecca prayed that it stayed that way because Diane could be the *worst*.

Rebecca had a full day ahead of her, so she went out of her way to get into the office by 5 a.m., and since Brandon was going to be shooting today, she figured she'd do some overtime as well.

Reading through horrible manuscripts mailed to the office was killing her. For new authors, Pretty & Bold Publications required all writers to mail in their manuscripts, but clearly, people didn't follow instructions. It sucked for them because if it wasn't from an author they were already working with, Rebecca would ignore it for the most part.

Some man had sent in a manuscript called *That Time I Fucked Your Mother,* and it wasn't like they were going to publish it, but Rebecca couldn't resist reading it. Just like the title, everything he had written was ignorant as ever, and the grammar was even worse.

"You look stressed." Diane came walking into Rebecca's office smiling from ear to ear.

"And you look like you've won the lotto," she replied.

"Well, in a way I have," she said, sitting down across from Rebecca.

"Spill it." Rebecca placed her highlighter down and put a sticky note on the manuscript page she was working on.

Noticing that Rebecca was more than halfway through the manuscript, Diane wondered how long she had been at work. It was only noon, and she usually didn't get into the office until 9 a.m., 8 at the earliest.

"Derek bought me a house…a *big*-ass house," Diane squealed.

"Stop playing. When did this happen?"

"Over the weekend. Nasir took me to look at a few houses, but this morning, he called to tell me that I can move in next week," Diane responded with excitement.

"That's amazing," Rebecca smiled. She was a bit thrown off by the mention of Nasir's name, but she wasn't mad; she knew that's how he made his living. She just wondered why Diane hadn't mentioned anything about it earlier.

"How is Nasir these days?"

Rebecca was curious to know what was going on with him. The last time they spoke, he was calling to let her know that it was Shantel who sent her the video as if that would make up for the pain he had caused. It didn't cancel out the fact that he cheated on her without hesitation.

"He looks good, and he has a baby boy on the way," Diane responded, unaware that Rebecca didn't know.

"Asshole!" she blurted out.

"…are you okay?"

"Um, I'm sorry, Diane…can you give me a minute please?" Rebecca felt herself about to have a breakdown.

"Take all the time you need. It looks like you've been working all day anyway," Diane said, getting up from her seat.

"Yeah, since 5 this morning."

Diane hugged Rebecca before she left her office, closing the door behind herself. Rebecca began to feel like she was losing control, and it terrified her. Unsure of what was going on with her body, she found herself underneath her desk short of breath, sweaty, and feeling like her heart was about to jump out of her chest. Closing her eyes, Rebecca tried to calm down, as she started to cry, but nothing was helping. Although she and Nasir were over, she found her heart breaking once again.

Thirty minutes later, she heard a knock on her office door.

"Who is it?" she called out, still sitting underneath her desk.

"…it's Nikki."

"Come in and *fast*," Rebecca replied.

Walking into the office, Nikki saw Rebecca's feet coming out from underneath her desk. Turning the corner, she found Rebecca holding onto her chest with mascara running down her face.

"Rebecca, what is going on?" Nikki sat down on the floor across from her and held onto her hands.

Wiping her face, Rebecca began to cry some more.

"…Na-Na-Nasir is having a baby with *that* bitch," she said, crying her eyes out. "What did she do to deserve a damn baby? I couldn't even have one of my own."

Nikki felt her pain, so she pulled her close and hugged her. Rebecca had been through so much, but this was just another blow she had to take. She lost her baby; she lost her fiancé, and now the man she lost to a *let's be friends* text was having a child with the woman he cheated on her with.

"It'll be okay. You have me, Monica, and a man at home who loves the ground you walk on," she said, kissing Rebecca's forehead. "This feeling will pass."

I sure hope so, Rebecca thought, as she rested her head on Nikki's shoulder.

45

Chapter Twelve
Regina & Shantel

"I am so happy to be off. You have no idea the day I've had."

"Work was busy like that?" Shantel asked.

When work ended, Regina decided to hit up happy hour at Chevy's with her baby sister. They hadn't been seeing each other much since she started dating Gary, and Shantel was still salty about Brandon friend-zoning her. She was doing everything possible to avoid him, which included spending time with her sister, but she couldn't help but miss him. For a while, she continued to shoot her shot by texting him here and there, liking his Instagram pictures, and calling him every chance she got, but he wasn't falling into her trap. Shantel didn't understand how going out of her way to break up Rebecca and Nasir led to Rebecca taking *her* man and Ashley getting a new house and baby.

"…*way* too busy. I took on Ashley's cases while she was on maternity leave, and I am tired."

"You are *too* nice." Shantel rolled her eyes. "What her fat-ass been doing?"

46

"Why are you so fucking rude? That's why nobody likes your ass but me," Regina said, shaking her head. "And if we weren't sisters, I probably wouldn't be your friend either."

"Well, bitch, that makes two of us, because I can't stand your stupid-ass either," Shantel snapped.

"Awww, don't get in your feelings."

As mean as Shantel was, she was sensitive as fuck.

"Anyway, Ashley is doing great, besides the little tension she and Nasir have been having over the shit you did," she said, giving her the side-eye.

"Don't be cutting your eyes at me. It's not my fault they got caught fucking," Shantel smirked.

"Bitch," Regina said, sipping her peach margarita, "we not even about to get into all that. Just know you messy as hell...what have you been doing though?"

"Besides running the club for Dad? Nothing, really."

All the showing off Shantel was doing around the city was catching up to her. The materialistic shit she was spending all her money on wasn't going to be able to keep up appearances if she didn't get her finances in order. Instead of going to their dad to ask for more money, she decided to ask him to teach her the trade. He thought she was joking for a minute because Shantel had never worked to earn anything a day in her life, but he was happy to teach her. That way when it came time to hand over his business, he knew he'd be able to trust her to keep his legacy going. Of course, he still wanted Regina to take care of all the financial aspects of his life though.

"How's that going?"

"Surprisingly better than I thought. The crowd is growing, and we've been having a lot more celebrity appearances, which means more money for *all* of us," Shantel smiled while rubbing her hands together.

"I'm happy to hear that. I'm going to have to come through one of these week-ends," Regina lied.

Since being with Gary, she didn't feel the need to be off in the clubs anymore. She had everything she wanted right in his arms. If she did go out, he'd be right along with her, and Shantel would throw a tantrum.

"Please do. You're going back to being boring-ass Becky now that your boo'd up," Shantel responded with a slight attitude.

"That's not what my man thinks," Regina laughed.

"Girl, bye," Shantel said, hugging Regina before heading out the door.

This little bitch would leave me with the bill.

48

Chapter Thirteen
Nikki & Monica

It had been another long day on set, but Monica was grateful for the chance to be on the big screen again. Being able to prove she took acting seriously made her feel accomplished. Most of the people in her life doubted her and placed a *gold-digger* label on her, which at one point, she was, but that's not what she wanted to be known for. Monica was willing to do anything to get on the winning team, but it took her almost losing her best friend to realize that some opportunities just aren't worth risking relationships with those you love.

For the last two months, Monica had been staying at Nikki's faithfully, only returning home to make sure the rent was paid and to grab extra clothes. Things between the two of them had been going so well that Monica was contemplating asking to move in. Since this was her first meaningful relationship, she didn't want to appear to be moving too quickly. She also knew that Nikki was still a little skeptical, being that the last woman she was with left her for a man.

Pulling into the parking garage, Monica was eager to get into the house to see her woman's smile, but when she finally walked through the door, she found Nikki sitting on the couch in the dark looking out of the window with a glass of wine in her hand.

"You ever sit back and wonder if any decisions you've made in life have affected someone else to the core?" Nikki asked as soon as the lights popped on.

Is she about to break up with me? Monica thought to herself before responding.

"…everything okay?" she asked, walking towards Nikki.

"I'm just thinking about how cruel some people can be," she responded before taking a sip of her wine.

"What are you talking about, crazy lady?"

"Nasir," Nikki said, caressing Monica's hand.

"I'm confused, babe. Why are you thinking about Nas? Is Rebecca talking to him again?"

It had been almost a year since Monica had seen Nasir, and Rebecca didn't bother bringing him up anymore. *Why is he topic of discussion suddenly?*

"Did you know that he has a baby due in like three months, or something like that?"

"No," Monica said, grabbing Nikki's face. "How do *you* know that?"

"Babe, I thought I'd seen Rebecca hurt before, but this was totally different. I thought I was going to have to take her to the hospital. She's in pain," Nikki continued, as she laid her head against Monica's chest.

50

"I'm calling her right now. Fuck him and that bitch," Monica said, reaching for her phone.

"Don't," Nikki uttered, as she snatched Monica's arm away.

"Why? She needs to cheer up and forget about that asshole."

"Because Rebecca doesn't need that kind of energy right now," Nikki said, shaking her head. "At this point, Rebecca doesn't even know if she can have kids of her own, so she's devastated."

"What do you mean she doesn't know if she can have kids?"

Monica and Rebecca had been friends forever, but they never talked about kids after she had that miscarriage with her ex-fiancé. Shit, Monica just figured she didn't want to have them anymore.

"Did you not know that she and Nasir tried to have a baby, but it never happened?" Nikki asked.

"I honestly had no clue. I'll give her some space, but we need to do something this weekend to help cheer her up."

"I agree," Nikki said, getting off the couch. "You want me to run you a bath?"

"No, I'm just going to hop in the shower, and then we can try to catch up on *This Is Us*."

Chapter Fourteen
Brandon

All week Rebecca had been confrontational with Brandon, and he wasn't sure how to handle it. Before they became a couple, everything between them had always been easy. Now that they were no longer friends, he couldn't force her to tell him what she was feeling. He knew that there was the potential of him pushing her away if he pushed too hard.

It was now Friday, and they hadn't had sex in four days, which wasn't normal for them. When he tried to get a quickie in, she yelled at him and then rushed out the door. Brandon had gotten used to making love to her almost daily, and now she was acting as if she could no longer stand to be around him.

Brandon had the day off and planned to leave all the directing in Gary's hands for the day, but with the way things were going at home, he figured he'd head over to set to see how things were going. Maybe, Monica could help him figure out what was going on.

Within an hour, Brandon arrived at the studio with coffee and donuts in hand.

"Good morning to the best crew there is," he said, putting on a fake smile.

"Good morning, boss," they all yelled back in unison.

"Um, so y'all just about to act like y'all like that fool more than me?" Gary scoffed, pretending to be jealous.

"You know I'm the nice one," Brandon said, placing the donuts and coffee down on the table.

"Well, on that note, I guess everyone can take a quick break," Gary yelled from the director's chair. "And hand me one of them donuts before you come over here," he said, looking at Brandon.

Brandon grabbed Gary a chocolate-covered donut with sprinkles, which was his favorite. Then, he grabbed a sugar donut and a caramel macchiato for himself before heading over to his brother.

"So, what's up?"

Gary knew his brother well enough to know that he didn't come all the way down to the studio on his day off for nothing.

"What you mean? I was just coming to see how production was coming along," Brandon lied.

"Yeah, okay. Everything on this side of town is going great. Monica is in the back getting her hair and makeup done now."

"Speaking of Monica," Brandon paused, "you think I can holla at her before y'all shoot that graduation party scene?"

"It's all good. Go back there now. You got about twenty minutes or so before I start putting all they asses back to work," he laughed. "You heard that everyone," he yelled out.

Walking to the back past wardrobe and hair & makeup, Monica was looking prettier than ever. Ever since they began filming, she had changed up her whole look to get into character. The long bright red weaves she would wear were long gone, and she colored her hair jet black.

"You look nice today," Brandon announced, as he entered the room.

Monica had on distressed mom jeans, with an oversized long-sleeved pinstriped shirt that hung off of her left shoulder. Her hair, which went to the middle of her back, was bumped at the ends, and her bangs were swooped to the right side of her face. The makeup she had on was flawless, to the point that you couldn't even tell that she had any on.

"I *always* look nice," she said, rolling her eyes.

"I'm just saying, you look like a natural beauty instead of a cast member off of *Love & Hip Hop*," he started to laugh.

"Fuck you, Brandon," she said, giving him the middle finger.

"Damn, is that any way to talk to your boss?" he asked, standing in front of her.

"No, but it is the way I talk to my best friend's sneaky-ass boyfriend."

Looking confused, Brandon excused everyone from the room so he could talk to

Monica in private. It was now clear that Rebecca was upset about something.

"What you mean 'sneaky'?" Brandon was leaning against the vanity with his arms folded.

Standing up, and looking at herself in the mirror, Monica began telling Brandon what was going on. She could tell that he was just as shocked about the whole baby situation as she was, but it now all made sense to Brandon why Rebecca was acting so weird all of a sudden.

"You know, she probably thinks you knew this whole time about Ashley being pregnant, with Nasir being your best friend and all," she said, running her fingers through her hair.

"I haven't spoken to him since me and Rebecca got serious. He only talks to Gary at this point," Brandon responded, realizing that Gary knew about the baby the whole time and said nothing.

"Well, me and Nikki are taking her out for drinks and karaoke tonight. I'll let her know that you had no idea. Maybe, she'll be ready to talk to you about it tomorrow...don't say anything about it for now."

"My lips are sealed."

Monica and Brandon shared a hug before she headed back to set to start shooting her scene. Brandon followed right behind her, trying to figure out how it was so easy for his brother to hide some shit like that from him. It was lightweight fucked up. He knew Gary was just trying to stay out of the middle of his and Nasir's drama…but *damn*.

"You cold," Brandon said, as he approached his brother. "A fucking baby?!"

Gary put his head down and shook it because he knew exactly what Brandon was talking about.

"Nasir didn't want me to say anything to you because of Rebecca. My bad, bro," he said, trying to give his brother some love.

"Yeah, okay, nigga. I see how it is," Brandon said, walking out of the studio.

Sitting in his car, Brandon thought about what Monica said about Rebecca thinking she was unable to conceive. He wanted to start a family with Rebecca, but it never crossed his mind that he may not be able to.

Chapter Fifteen
Rebecca

"I'm heading out. I need to go meet Derek, so we can finish getting the rest of my house packed up for the move," Diane announced, as she walked into Rebecca's office.

"Anything you need me to do?" Rebecca asked, hoping she'd say "yes".

For the first time, she wished that she was swamped with work, so she could stay behind at the office for a few more hours.

"Nope, I've got it all handled," she said, turning around to leave, but, suddenly, she stopped in her tracks. "Oh and take the day off Monday. I'm closing the office for the day."

Oh, this bitch is in a good mood.

"Have a good weekend and let me know if you need any help moving," Rebecca smiled, as she waved goodbye.

Looking at the clock, it was going on 4 p.m., and she didn't have much work to do anyway. She figured she'd pack up and head home as well. She was supposed to be meeting Nikki and Monica at the house for a girl's night, one that was *much* needed.

57

Shutting down her computer, Rebecca grabbed her keys, and locked up her office so none of those nosy bitches in the office would find themselves chilling in her chair like she used to do when Diane was gone, then she headed to the elevator.

"Any plans for the weekend, Miss Rebecca?"

"Hey, Laura…I'm just going to hang out with my best friend and maybe record a podcast. Nothing too fancy," she responded, stepping into the elevator. "You have a good weekend, and I'll see you Tuesday."

I wish that girl would let me be sometimes, she thought, as she waited for the door to close.

Laura was a 22-year-old graphic designer, who started working for them about two months ago. With things at the company getting very busy, Diane decided to hold a contest to find the best new graphic designers fresh out of college in L.A. County, and Laura was runner-up. To Rebecca's surprise, she ended up being a fan of her vlog *Rebecca Loves a Read* and tried to find every chance she could to speak with her about…*absolutely* nothing.

Jumping into her new all-black 2018 BMW X5 that Brandon bought her, she rolled down all the windows and let her hair down. Pulling out of the parking garage, she began to smile as "Get You" by Daniel Caesar began to play.

Rebecca's hair blew in the wind as she sang along to her and Brandon's song. *Gosh, I've been such a bitch.*

"Dial, Bae B."

"Dialing Bae B," Siri responded on the Bluetooth.

Brandon picked up on the first ring, which didn't surprise Rebecca. He was always thrilled to hear from her.

"Hey, babe. How was your day?" he asked with excitement in his voice.

"It was good. I have a three-day weekend…maybe, we can do something special," Rebecca suggested. "I also wanted to talk to you about me being so distant lately."

"Whatever you want; your wish is my command…love you, and I'll see you at home," he replied.

"I love you too."

Rebecca hung up the phone and was in a better mood than she was before she left the house.

Maybe, this girl's night won't be as bad as I thought.

Arriving home almost an hour later, Rebecca stopped in front of the house to grab the mail and then pulled into the driveway. Before getting out of the car, she began looking through the mail to see if anything of importance had come for her. Instead, she came across an invitation addressed to *The Lovely Couple* from *Ashley*.

This bitch!

Walking into the house, Rebecca found Brandon sitting on the couch with a beer in hand, watching the news.

I guess it's time to talk, she thought to herself, as she continued to look at the envelope.

"...we have mail," she said, walking over to Brandon and sitting on his lap

"Addressed to the both of us?" he asked, sitting up to kiss her neck.

"You won't believe who it's from."

Handing him the envelope, still looking at Ashley's name in disgust, Rebecca leaned back and watched as he opened it. There was a picture of a lion sitting on a throne that read:

Oh, boy! Our Prince is on the way. Please join us to celebrate Nasir Wright Jr. Saturday, Feb. 1st, 2-6 p.m. RSVP with Ashley & Nasir for the address.

"Wow," Brandon said, shaking his head and throwing the invite down on the table.

"...you didn't know?" Rebecca asked in disbelief.

"That's exactly what I've been trying to tell you. Now, you can believe me, or we can fight about it," he said, before wrapping his arms around her waist.

"I just thought..."

"You just thought because Gary still fucks with that nigga that I knew he had a baby on the way with that crazy-ass broad," he said, cutting her off. "Well, guess what...?

My damn brother left me in the dark, so this is new to me like it is you."

Rebecca felt stupid for taking her issues out on Brandon, knowing that he and Nasir were no longer friends. She felt guilty for even caring about whether he was having a baby or not. It wasn't like they were friends, and she damn sure wasn't sending any congratulations Ashley's way.

"I'm sorry, babe," she said, leaning down to kiss him.

"Does it bother you that he isn't having a baby with you? Because if it does...maybe, we shouldn't be together."

Brandon wasn't about to sit around knowing the woman he wanted to marry was just using him to get over her ex. If they were going to be in this relationship, he needed to know that she was in it for the right reasons.

"Of course not. I want to be with you. I...I just got triggered when I heard the news from Diane is all," she said, placing her hands on his face. "I'm not sure if I can have kids, Brandon."

Taking his thumb, he wiped the tear that was making its way down Rebecca's cheek and pulled her close.

"Have you even checked to see?"

"No, but I'm sure I can't."

"You won't know until we try, and I know that we are going to have a child together because we are meant to be," Brandon said before grabbing Rebecca's face and kissing her passionately.

"I love you," she said, pulling back a little.

"I love you more."

Chapter Sixteen
Rebecca & The Girls

Rebecca was smiling from ear to ear, and every worry she felt had washed away with every kiss Brandon laid upon her face, down to her thick thighs. The moment he entered her paradise, she did not doubt that one day, they'd create life, just like he said, but she was in no rush. Rebecca wanted to continue enjoying what the two of them had together.

Nikki and Monica had arrived to pick her up in the middle of them making love on the couch, so they had to wait in the car for a good thirty minutes.

"Still mesmerized over that dick you got before we left the house?" Monica laughed.

"She's *definitely* in a better mood," Nikki added.

"Oh, shut up," Rebecca blushed. "I haven't felt his touch all week, and it was needed."

"As long as you're happy, we're happy," Nikki said, getting out of the Uber and entering Boardwalk 11, a Karaoke Bar & Grill. She and Monica figured it would be the best place to take Rebecca. They had amazing food, and good drinks, and although, it got crowded, the folks there were always chill and fun to be around. It wasn't your typical karaoke place where you'd rent a room and enjoy songs with just your friends. You had to have some balls to get up in front of a room full of strangers.

They decided to get there by at least 6 p.m., so they could enjoy happy hour, but since Rebecca was too busy having makeup sex, they didn't make it until 8 p.m., just in time to see people make a fool of themselves.

Grabbing a seat in the last booth, the ladies got comfortable and waited for their waiter to come to take their order. Rebecca had barely eaten all week, and if she knew any better, she needed to get some food in her system before Nikki and Monica got her fucked up. Rebecca knew that was the only reason they took an Uber.

"Can I get you ladies started with a drink and an appetizer?" asked a tall, white guy with blonde hair and green eyes.

"You can start us with an order of buffalo wings, French fries, and onion rings," Rebecca said, looking at Nikki and Monica for approval. "I'd also like a regal apple sour."

"And for you, ladies?"

"Bring us six shots of your best vodka…and that'll be all," Monica smiled.

"Oh, you trying to get drunk drunk, huh?" Rebecca laughed.

"I think we deserve it," Monica said, directing her attention towards the karaoke stage.

The DJ was killing it with some classics and the newest hits. No one was standing up to get on the mic just yet, but Monica knew once everyone got a little liquor in them, they'd be ready to sing their hearts out.

"So, are you going to tell us what happened with you and Brandon?" Nikki was curious to see how their conversation went.

Just as Rebecca was about to get into the details, the waiter came back with their drinks.

"Here you go, ladies. Your appetizers will be out shortly," he said, placing the shot glasses down on the table.

Once he was gone, Nikki picked up her shot, and Rebecca and Monica followed suit.

"…here's to friendship and love."

"*Ugh,*" Rebecca blurted out, making the ugliest face after she threw her shot back. Shots were not her thing.

"*Sooooo?*" Nikki responded, waiting to hear the scoop.

"Girl, so when I got home, there was an envelope addressed to me and Brandon…from fucking Ashley," Rebecca said, rolling her eyes.

"Now, you know the minute I saw that I wanted to go in that house and go the hell off."

"Well, why didn't you? You know if it was me, it would be another story," Monica said, already knowing that Brandon had no clue about the baby. Rebecca didn't know she knew, and there was no reason for her to.

"Because he was just as shocked as I was. He almost went off on *me* when I questioned him about it," Rebecca said, taking down the second shot sitting in front of her. Right as she put the glass down, she looked up, only to see Shantel walking in her direction with Regina in tow.

"...who the fuck invited her?"

Chapter Seventeen
Shantel

"If it isn't the girl everyone loves—little Miss Rebecca."

Shantel pushed her way into the booth next to Nikki like she owned the place, and Monica was ready to jump across the table and snatch that bun right off her head.

"Bitch, you *can* say, 'excuse me,'" Nikki said, shoving Shantel. "Why the fuck are you even over here?"

"If you'd like to know…me and my sister come here a lot, and I just so happened to see you guys over here looking like the miserable bitches you are, so I thought I'd come say, 'hello,'" Shantel smirked.

"I see why Brandon stopped dealing with your bitter ass," Rebecca said, sipping her drink.

"Who the fuck are you calling 'bitter'?" Shantel asked, jumping out of her seat.

"The bitch with the bun on her head and a $2 outfit."

Nikki and Monica burst out in laughter, and you could see the rage in Shantel's eyes, but there was nothing she could do about it. If she even took one step towards Rebecca, she knew she'd be getting the crap beat out of her before she could even blink twice.

"Nothing to say?"

Just as Rebecca was about to proceed to go off on Shantel, she saw Regina coming her way.

"Oh, hey, Regina," Rebecca smiled, as she approached. "I was just telling your sister how lovely she looks."

"You're always so sweet. That's why I love you," she responded, as she gave the girls each a hug.

"You know, I try my best….would you like to sit with us? I was just talking to the girls about Ashley's baby shower."

Rebecca put on the fakest act she could, and the look on Shantel's face was to die for. You could tell she hated not being the center of attention. Shantel didn't intimidate Rebecca one bit though, and it was pissing her off.

"We're already waiting for a table," Shantel snapped.

"Really? I couldn't tell by the way you came over here welcoming yourself to our booth," Rebecca smiled.

"We'd love to sit with you," Regina mentioned. "I haven't been able to see you since the twins started production on that film. I heard you've been doing great by the way, Monica."

I know, she thought to herself and smiled.

"So, you're going to sit down with this fake-ass bitch?" Shantel asked, still standing there with her arms folded.

This was supposed to be their night together, yet Regina wanted to play catchup with Rebecca. Sometimes, Shantel wished her sister was still depressed over what happened with her fiancé; at least then, she knew she'd get to spend time with her. Now, here she was practically living with Gary and buddy-buddy with her ex's new girlfriend.

"Sit your ass down and stop being such a brat," Regina snapped at Shantel. "This is exactly why no one likes you."

"Says the bitch who couldn't tell her *so-called* friend that Nasir was having a baby," Shantel shot back.

"It wasn't my place to tell," Regina said, looking at Rebecca. "But I see Ashley sent you an invite like she said she would."

"Does Nasir know we're invited?" Rebecca asked.

"If we're being honest, I don't think he does, but Ashley was tired of hiding her pregnancy and thought that if Gary could be there then why shouldn't Brandon?"

"Just like a nigga, still keeping secrets from someone he isn't even with," Monica added.

"Who gives a fuck? I'm going home, Regina. I can't wait until Gary cheats on your ass and these bitches cut you loose," Shantel said, giving the girls the middle finger.

"So angry, this one," Nikki laughed.

Before Shantel could say anything else, Regina slapped the fuck out of her.

"Just because you couldn't keep Brandon doesn't give you the right to take your anger out on me and everyone else at this table. Learn to grow the fuck up, Shantel."

"Um, can we get some more shots please?" Rebecca yelled as she waved the waiter over.

"Whatever, I'm out," Shantel said, quickly turning to walk away.

Chapter Eighteen
Gary & Nasir

Filming for the day ended earlier than expected, so Gary decided to go home and take a nap, which was unusual for him. But since being with Regina, he did everything he could to make sure he stayed out of the clubs and the streets. Right now, he was as loyal as he knew how to be, and he even went as far as changing his number. Gary didn't want any of his old things reaching out and jeopardizing what he and Regina had. Even though she wasn't as nasty in the bedroom as he would've liked, she had everything else going for her.

Instead of hitting the bar, Gary decided to hit up Nasir and see if he was down for a late-night run along the beach. Seeing him also allowed him to catch him up on what was going on with Brandon.

Putting on his Apple watch and Nike Windrunners, Gary grabbed his keys and headed out the door to meet Nasir in Santa Monica at the Strand Beach Path, which was one of his favorite nighttime destinations.

Gary:

71

Hey, babe, heading to Santa Monica to meet Nasir for a run. Let me know when you get back home.

Regina:
Have a great run. Love you!

Gary:
Love you too.

This girl really got me checking in, he thought, as he went to Apple Music and turned on 6LACK.

Regina:
Oh, by the way, I'm with Rebecca right now, and I just found out that Ashley invited her and Brandon to the baby shower.

"Now ain't that some shit," Gary said aloud.

About forty minutes into Gary's ride, he was parking down by the Santa Monica Pier where he said he would meet Nasir. The path was about forty miles, but since it was late, they were only going to run about five. That was enough time to tell Nasir about Brandon and maybe get him to agree to reconcile.

Walking toward the entrance of the pier, Gary spotted Nasir stretching. He was ready to get going, so he stretched by his car, and he still had a bit of a way to walk to get to Nasir.

"...long time no see," Nasir joked since he had just seen Gary at the gym a few days prior. Instead of drinking partners, they were now workout partners, which was once Nasir's and Brandon's thing.

"Awww, miss me?" Gary asked. "Let's go. We got some shit to talk about," he continued, as he jogged in place.

That can't be good, Nasir thought, as they started their run.

"Everything good with you, bruh?"

"Shit, I can't complain. Making this movie that's probably going to make me millions and got a woman I'm being faithful to," Gary laughed. "Life is great."

"You and Gina really been going strong. I thought she would've been left yo' ass."

"You got jokes," Gary said, shaking his head.

"…a few."

Pausing the conversation for a while to catch their breath, Gary let the breeze brush across his face, moving out of the way of the few bikers speeding down the path. The air smiled like the ocean, and they could hardly see, besides the glare from the moon glowing on the water. Gary wanted to talk to Nasir, but he figured he'd wait until they headed back towards the pier.

"Ready to head back before we go too far in?" Nasir asked, breaking the silence between the two of them. "I know you aren't in shape like you used to be."

"And he shoots again," Gary said, turning around.

Five miles later, Gary was lying across the pavement holding his chest. "Damn, I'm old," he said, sitting up slowly.

"You act like it," Nasir laughed. "But what's up? I know you didn't ask me out here for no reason," he said, sitting down next to him.

Here we go, Gary thought to himself.

"...it's about Brandon."

"What about him?"

"He knows about the baby. Ashley sent him and Rebecca an invitation to the baby shower. I can tell he wasn't too happy with me holding that secret from him."

Gary was letting it all out.

"On top of that, I feel like it's time for you and him to sit down and talk. This shit is getting old, and I'm tired of being in the middle of y'all's shit. Eventually, I'm going to have to choose, and you know I have to go with blood."

"Man, I'm not the one who decided to wife up my homie's ex," Nasir responded, not wanting to hear what Gary was saying.

"Bruh, let's be real. From the day you introduced those two, they had a chemistry that couldn't be matched. You let the two of them get too close. I know you don't want to hear it, but you basically set them up to be together," Gary shrugged.

"So, you trying to say I ran my girl into the arms of a nigga who was *supposed* to be my brother?" Nasir was getting irritated and was ready to go.

"That's *exactly* what I'm saying. If you didn't fuck around with Ashley, Rebecca wouldn't have gone and found comfort under B. It is what it is."

Nasir got up and was getting ready to walk away.

"Have you even been able to enjoy this pregnancy with Ashley?" Gary stood up to face Nasir.

"What does that have to do with anything?"

"It has a lot to do with everything. You're spending all this time worried about Brandon and Rebecca, that you probably haven't put any effort into the relationship you have now," Gary said, getting real with Nasir.

Everyone was so used to Gary being the joker of the group that they barely listened to anything he had to say, but Nasir couldn't deny that Gary was speaking all facts. It had been a year since he and Rebecca ended their relationship, yet he was still mad at her for not giving him a second chance, not like he deserved one. On top of that, he was still treating Ashley like one of his sidepieces. Sure, he moved her into a nice house and was providing her with everything she needed, but he was still hiding her from the world, trying his best to protect Rebecca's feelings.

Maybe, it is time to have a sit down with Brandon and let shit go.

"Man," Nasir said, shaking his head. "When's the next time you linking up with B?"

"Sunday. We were going to have a movie night at his place. Come through?"

"Nah, I know y'all women going to be there. This needs to be a brother-only conversation. Set that up, and I'll be there."

"Bet," Gary said hugging Nasir. "It's been too long."

Yeah, it has, Nasir thought, as he headed to his car.

Chapter Nineteen
Ashley & Nicole

As usual, Ashley was spending another Saturday alone. Nasir
worked so much at this point that
she thought he was staying occupied at work
just to get away from her, but she didn't have
the energy to fight for his affection any
longer. Once the baby came, things would
possibly be different, but until then, she was
going to accept their issues and how they
came.

Getting out of their king-sized bed, Ashley walked over to the window to take in the
view of the city; it was what she liked most
about their home. No matter the time of day
or the weather, she always had the perfect
scenery. Today, the sky was clear and blue,
with a slight breeze.

Walking into the kitchen, she saw a plate
of breakfast on the table, a bottle of Marti-
nelli's apple juice, a vase of white roses, and
a note addressed to her from Nasir.

To the love of my life,

*Sorry for the distance and all the secrecy. As the
mother of my child and the woman I plan to spend
my life with, you deserve nothing but the best and to*

77

be treated like nothing less. Tonight, I have something special planned. Be out front at 7 p.m. There will be a driver waiting for you. Don't worry about what to wear; I've already got it handled. Check the closet…but after you eat.

Sincerely,
Your Forever Love

"He loves me," Ashley said to herself, as she grabbed her plate to warm the food.

I wonder what he has planned…

Sitting down at the table, she ate her French toast, potatoes, and bacon within twenty minutes. After clearing off the table, she washed the remaining dishes sitting in the sink. Ashley hated a dirty house.

Heading back into the room, she walked into the bathroom to run herself a bubble bath. She had gotten to the point of her pregnancy where she could barely stand, so a bath was always her best bet. While the water ran, she made up the bed and plugged in her oil diffuser to fill the room with the smell of lavender. Ashley was doing all she could to stay relaxed and in a good head space.

Walking back into the bathroom, she turned off the water and slipped off her robe. Looking at herself in the mirror, she turned to the side and rubbed her stomach.

"I can't believe you're mine."

Ashley spent a good forty minutes in the bathroom before recalling that she needed to hurry and get dressed to go meet Nicole at the outdoor venue she was planning to have her wedding in late July.

Walking into her closet, which Nasir had personally made for her, she saw an all-black dress and a pair of custom-made sandals.

How thoughtful, she smiled.

Ashley's feet had been swelling like crazy, and she could barely fit into any shoes, let alone heels. Nasir was paying more attention to her more than she thought.

Throwing on an oversized hoodie, jogger pants, and her favorite pair of Nikes, she went into the bathroom to lay her edges. Throughout this whole pregnancy, she managed to keep her hair appointments, because she refused to let her hair get too long. Everyone told her to get braids, but she didn't have the patience to sit in a chair for eight hours.

Applying the last of her makeup so she wouldn't look a total mess in public, Ashley ordered a Lyft and let her sister know that she'd be on the way soon. The ride was going to be somewhat expensive, but there was no way she was driving herself to Malibu.

"...we're here," Ashley's driver announced an hour later, as they approached the Sunset Restaurant.

"Thank God," she mumbled under her breath.

"What was that?"

"…just thanking you for getting me here unharmed. Have a wonderful day," she said, as she got out.

The man who picked her up was unusually awkward, and he talked non-stop. From the moment he arrived in her driveway, she wanted to call another Lyft, but she had no time. He asked about her due date, and if she was with the child's father, went on about his failed relationships, and wouldn't stop telling her how pretty she was.

"This place is beautiful," she said to herself, as she walked inside to find Nicole.

"Right on time," Nicole said, waving her over. "The planner was just about to show us the outdoor patio and the spot we'll be saying our vows."

"I still can't believe my baby sister is getting married *before* me," Ashley said, hugging her.

"I'm sure you and Nasir are next."

"*Hmm*, I don't know," she said, following behind a short blonde lady with a book full of wedding décor.

"While you and your lovely bridal party are over there in the sugary sand taking pics in front of the alluring water where you hopefully get a few dolphins," the planner said, pointing towards the water, "your guests will be on this patio enjoying cocktails and appetizers until you are ready to make your way inside for the reception and main course."

"I love it! I know everything will be beautiful with the all-white décor and lavender flowers," Nicole smiled from ear to ear.

"Have you figured out your final guest count yet?" the planner asked, pulling out her notebook.

"I think we'll have about 100 to 120 guests, and for the reception, there will probably be 200," Nicole responded, as they walked back inside.

"Sounds perfect! And do you still want to add LED starlight on the patio area?"

"Yes. I will email you a few pictures later of how I'd like the reception area to look," Nicole said, grabbing her purse.

"Talk to you soon." The planner smiled and hugged them goodbye.

When Nicole reached down to grab her purse, Ashley noticed bruises around her sister's wrist, much like what she would see when she was younger. Since Nicole was so excited about today, Ashley didn't want to ruin the moment by asking questions, but it was something they were going to have to talk about. If Derek was putting his hands on her, they had no business walking down the aisle.

"So, you know I need a ride, right?" Ashley said, following behind Nicole.

"You lucky you my sister, and I don't have to rush home to my man," she laughed.

"…speaking of," Ashley said, looking at her sister. "Why wasn't he here today?"

"If you *must* know," Nicole said, getting into the car, "he was busy."

"Busy doing what? Has he even seen the venue yet?"

"Helping his friend move into his new house. It's not a big deal. He knows I have everything handled." Nicole was getting defensive.

"If you say so," Ashley shrugged, looking out the window. "Let me know when we get home."

Ashley let her eyes close and drifted away to sleep. She had a bad feeling about this guy Derek, and the way Nicole was ready to throw her out, she knew something was up, but it wasn't her place to talk about it. Nicole was no longer a child, and she had the right to do what she wanted to do. Ashley had other things to worry about, like fixing her relationship with Nasir and making sure her baby was good.

Chapter Twenty
Ashley & Nasir

When Ashley got home, she had two hours to get ready and be out the door. Not wanting to stuff her face before meeting Nasir, she grabbed an apple and some peanut butter to snack on before jumping in the shower.

Looking in the mirror, she felt like the most beautiful woman walking on earth, wearing the black fitted dress Nasir had bought her. She hadn't noticed the split up the side, but it was perfect, as it gave her thick thighs the freedom to move.

It had been a while since she had gotten dressed up, let alone gone on a date. Nasir was either always too busy with work, or Ashley was too busy being mad, but, tonight, she was delighted to see what he had planned for her.

Grabbing her phone, which was sitting on the marble countertop next to her makeup bag, Ashley walked to the full-length mirror and began to take pictures of herself.

Nasir:
Remember, 7 on the dot.

"Oh, shit," Ashley yelled out, as she rushed into her closet to grab her shoes and light pink fur coat. It was already 6:40 p.m., and she still needed to brush her teeth and finish her makeup.

Ashley:
Applying my lipstick now.

At exactly 7, Ashley was locking the door behind herself and being greeted by a tall, handsome, black man standing in front of an all-black G-Class Mercedes-Benz.

"Hello, Mrs. Wright. You look lovely," he said, opening the back door.

Mrs. Wright?

Ashley thought about correcting him, but she liked the sound of it. She didn't see anything wrong with being Nasir's wife for the night.

Grabbing the driver's hand, he helped her into the car and closed the door once she was securely inside.

"I'll be taking you to your destination...any music requests?" he asked before pulling off.

"Sade please!"

Hopping on the 101, Ashley wondered where they were headed. She asked the driver three times, but all he kept saying was, "I can't provide you that information, Mrs. Wright."

About twenty-five minutes later, they were pulling up to a tall beige building in the center of Downtown L.A., and Nasir was patiently waiting outside for her.

Opening Ashley's door, he had the smile of a man who didn't want to be anywhere else in the world.

"Follow me, my love," he said, grabbing her by the hand. "You look beautiful in that dress."

"Thank you," she responded, following Nasir into the elevator.

As they stepped inside, he placed a blindfold over her eyes. He wanted everything to be a surprise. Nasir had put this night together in a short time, but because of his spotless reputation, he was able to get ahold of the manager of the building and rent the rooftop area for the rest of the night. It set his pockets back $10,000, but it was going to be worth it to see the smile on Ashley's face.

Making their way up to the 15th floor, Nasir guided Ashley out of the elevator and removed her blindfold.

"Oh, my god." Ashley's eyes were bright and wide. "This place is beautiful."

"I was hoping you'd like it. One day, I'll show you what France really looks like," he said, pulling her close.

"Where is everyone?" Ashley looked around and noticed that the place was empty, besides those who were there to serve them.

"Hello, Mr. Wright! You and the Mrs. can follow me out to the patio," said a slender Italian man in a suit.

As they walked outside, Ashley took in the downtown skyline view; the stars above sparkled like diamonds.

They were seated at a beautiful antique table in front of a fireplace. There were pink roses on the table and her favorite lavender candles. Nasir even had their orders planned out, so she wouldn't waste time looking over the menu. The minute they sat down, waiters were bringing out food.

They started with French onion soup, chicken Caesar salad, house chips served with pesto aioli, and grilled filet and shrimp skewers. For the main course, Nasir had the chef serve bacon mac & cheese, pan-seared salmon with veggies, potatoes, and steak. Ashley was in food heaven and wished she could eat it all, but then she would be popping out her gown before Nasir got a chance to take it off.

"Thank you for this," Ashley said, reaching over the table to hold his hand. "I needed a night like this. We haven't been on the best of terms, but this shows me that you want to make it work."

"You deserve to have a night like this…and it's not over."

Nasir got up from his seat, walked over to Ashley, and grabbed her by the hand to help her up. For a moment, he paused and placed his hands on her stomach to say "hi" to his junior.

"Did you feel that?" he asked with excitement in his voice.

"I sure did. That little boy better calm the hell down," Ashley said, placing her hand on her stomach too.

"He's just excited to hear my voice," Nasir smiled.

"I see."

Ashley continued to follow Nasir as they made their way into the elevator, which took them to the top floor. As soon as the door opened, Ashley was greeted by a man with a bouquet and a rose petal carpet lined with candles. The minute the elevator doors closed, a band began to play Ashley's favorite song— "No Ordinary Love" by Sade.

"Can I have this dance?" Nasir asked, walking her to the center of the rooftop.

"Of course, you can."

Nasir pulled Ashley in as close as he could without feeling like he was hurting his son; he was always scared about putting too much pressure on her stomach. Wrapping her arms around his neck, Ashley looked around at the city lights and up at the stars surrounding them. She felt like she was living out a scene of every girl's favorite romance; all she needed was for Nasir to get down on one knee, and her night would be complete.

"I have to tell you something," she said, looking up at Nasir.

"It's okay…I already know about the invite, but I need you to stop going behind my back. If we're going to be in this, we need to communicate better," he said, kissing her on the forehead.

"I love you, Nasir."

"I love you too," he responded, placing his hand on her stomach once again. "When we get home, I have to tell you something."

"About?"

"About that nigga your sister is marrying," he said, shaking his head.

"…I fucking *knew* it."

Chapter Twenty-One
Movie Day

" Babe, you won't believe who I saw last night."

"Would you like me to guess...?" Brandon asked as he set up the movies in the theater room.

The couple would be arriving soon, and he wanted to make sure that he had everything ready. The movies for the day were *Two Can Play That Game, The Brothers,* and Rebecca's favorite, *B.A.P.S.* They were getting a little bit of everything—comedy, romance, and drama. It was something they could all enjoy without someone complaining about how much they couldn't stand the acting or the storyline.

"Nope," Rebecca responded, setting up the drinks and snacks. "It was your little ghetto-ass girlfriend."

"Now, you know the only girlfriend I got is you...and you're far from ghetto," he laughed.

"You know I'm talking about that Shantel bitch," Rebecca said, rolling her eyes. "What did you see in her anyway? She's so damn miserable."

"Ass," Brandon whispered.

"Excuse me?" Rebecca quickly turned around, but before she could say anything, the doorbell rang.

Saved by the bell, Brandon thought, as he ran up the steps to answer the door.

He better be glad there's somebody at that door, she thought, as she dipped her chip in some salsa.

"*Pizza's here!*" Brandon came yelling, as he walked out of the elevator with Monica and Nikki behind him.

"I think she can hear your loud-ass," Monica said, pushing past Brandon.

"He's being obnoxious because I brought up his loudmouth girlfriend," Rebecca said, walking over to Monica to hug her.

She and Nikki had on matching Nike sweatsuits, looking like the cutest lesbian couple Rebecca had ever seen.

"Man, Brandon," Nikki said, shaking her head, "I was ready to beat her ass. That girl has some fucking nerve."

"Stop playing." He grabbed a slice of pizza, then walked over to his reclining chair next to Rebecca.

"She's not playing," Rebecca laughed. "Nikki pushed her ass out the booth so hard."

"Why was she even sitting with you?"

Brandon was curious to find out how the rest of the night went before Gary showed up with Regina. He already knew they had run into Shantel when they were out because she had begun to blow up his phone the minute she left the bar. From the moment he answered the phone, he regretted it. Brandon didn't even know why he unblocked her in the first place.

Shantel immediately voiced how she ran into Rebecca and how she didn't deserve to be with him. Before she could say anything else, Brandon ended the conversation and told her not to call him again. Of course, that didn't stop her from sending him a picture of her ass, but Brandon deleted all traces of the conversation before Rebecca got back home, but not before taking a few more glimpses at the picture she sent.

Doesn't hurt to look, he thought.

"I guess her and Regina were having a sisters' night at the same spot. That ended quickly when Shantel said some shit about hoping Gary cheats on her," Rebecca responded. "Regina was pissed."

"The bitch is bitter," Monica said, coming to sit down after grabbing her snacks.

"No lie, she's been that way since high school—a straight-up bitch for no reason, and that's exactly why I couldn't take her ass serious."

"Anyway, enough about her…where's your brother?"

Rebecca was ready to get the movies started. They were already thirty minutes late, and they didn't have all night to be waiting around. She needed to be at work early so she could get through the final edits of the newest book they were going to release, and she still needed to run some ideas by Nikki for their podcast.

"I'll give him a call. You, ladies, can start watching *B.A.P.S. because* I know that's what you're dying to put on. I'll be right back." Brandon kissed Rebecca on the forehead before he made his way out of the room.

He knows me so well, she thought, as she watched him walk away.

Each day that passed, he became more attracted to Rebecca, and she couldn't help but be mesmerized by him.

Heading up the elevator and into the living room, Brandon plopped down on the couch to call up Gary. He was still irritated with him for hiding that Nasir was having a kid; they were supposed to be closer than that. He felt played by his brother, so he couldn't care less if he showed up or not.

As the phone began to ring, he heard the doorbell.

"That's me," Gary responded and then hung up.

Opening the door, Brandon gave Regina a hug and Gary a fake "hello" before trying to hurry back down to the movie room.

"Aye, can I talk to you real quick?" Gary asked before he sat down on the couch.

"Wassup, bruh?" Brandon turned back around. "The girls already started watching *B.A.P.S.*"

"Oooh, that's my movie," Regina said, kissing Gary and then turning around to run to the elevator.

"It's not going to take long. We need to just have a quick discussion about Nasir and this baby shower situation."

"What about it?" Brandon asked, frustrated.

"It's time to get this shit worked out before Saturday comes rolling around."

"Man..." Brandon walked towards Gary to take a seat himself. "This nigga could have talked to me a long time ago, but he wants to be hella childish."

"Well, you did swoop in on his girl before he could even attempt to get her back," Gary had to remind him.

"I know you're my brother and all, but that was fucked up."

"It's over and done with now. He just needs to focus on Ashley and the baby they have coming, instead of him wishing Rebecca was still on his arm."

"Fuck all that shit. We're all brothers, and it's time to fix shit. So, tomorrow after we shoot, we're about to meet at the Bar & Grill downtown like we used to and get shit back to what it should be, all right?" Gary patted Brandon on the shoulder.

"I guess," he said, getting up and thinking of all the ways shit could go wrong. He and Nasir hadn't talked in almost a year; shit was going to be awkward as hell.

Chapter Twenty-Two
Derek

Derek lay in Diane's California king-sized bed, covered in white silk sheets and matching comforter as he looked up at the ceiling. It was almost time for him to get back to his lady, but he didn't want to leave the woman he was lying next to. Derek was happy and had fallen in love, but it was all happening at the wrong time. If he knew he was going to run into his soul mate one day, he wouldn't have asked Nicole to marry him.

He felt like his hopes and dreams of settling down were coming to an end, so he jumped at the idea of marriage with anyone he thought would say "yes". Now, he was stuck trying to figure out how to end things with Nicole. Part of him hoped that she would catch him spending every weekend away from home while ignoring her calls for hours, but she hadn't.

Rolling over, Derek wrapped his arms around Diane and pulled her close. She could feel his manhood, so she snuggled up to him a little more and placed her hand on top of his.

"I have to get ready to go," he said, kissing her neck.

"Why do you always have to leave?"

Diane turned around to face him with a sad look on her face. She was tired of him coming over every Friday night and leaving first thing Sunday morning. The only reason she picked out the house they were in was that she thought he'd be in it with her...permanently.

Diane had it all figured out; all she was waiting for was the proposal she had always dreamed of.

"You know it's easier for me to focus on my cases in my own space," he said, feeling like shit for lying.

"I know. I know. But you know how much I love having you around. Plus, it gets lonely in this huge place."

"You won't be for long," Derek responded with a big smile on his face.

"I pray," Diane said, wrapping her hand around his dick.

Derek enjoyed sleeping in the nude, which made it easy for her to take advantage when she wanted to.

Stroking his shaft with one hand, Diane used her other to massage her breast.

"I promise," Derek said before kissing her passionately.

Placing his hand underneath her nightgown to spread her legs, he rolled over on top of her, kissing and sucking on her neck, while massaging her insides with his fingers. Letting out soft moans, Diane started to grind up and down on his fingers. Feeling her love come down, Derek put his head under the sheets, spread her legs wide, and started to make love to her with his tongue.

"Right there," Diane moaned, as he sucked up all her juices.

"You ready for this dick?" he asked, as he came up to kiss her lips.

He loved how she enjoyed tasting her juices after he sucked the soul out of her.

Not saying a word, Diane grabbed his dick and slowly inserted it inside of her. They locked into one another, and Derek stroked her nice and slow; it was like their bodies were one. With every stroke, Diane matched his pace, squirting every time he hit her G-spot. The bed was covered in her love, but it didn't stop Derek from making her flood the sheets.

Taking control, Diane got on top of Derek and began to bounce up and down on his dick as she grinded her hips back and forth, making his eyes roll in the back of his head.

"Fuck," he mouthed, squeezing Diane tight as he came.

"You sure you can't stay a little longer?" she asked, laying on his chest, as they both tried to catch their breath.

"Maybe just a little," he said, closing his eyes, and drifting back to sleep.

Two hours later, Derek woke up to a homecooked meal and a phone full of missed calls from Nicole.

She's going to kill me!

Derek ate the hamburger and fries Diane had cooked for him and then took a shower. He couldn't waste any more time living a fake fairytale life. He had to get home and be sure that his story was figured out before he walked through the front door.

Diane had a slight tantrum before he left, but Derek planned to fix that by making sure an Edible Arrangement and flowers were at her desk before she arrived at work in the morning.

Speeding down the freeway, Derek thought about every possible reaction Nicole would have to him being gone all weekend...*again*. She had been planning this extravagant wedding, while he was building a life with another woman.

Stopping at the grocery store on his way, Derek grabbed some flowers, a bottle of wine, chocolate, strawberries, whipped cream, and some popcorn. He figured he'd spend a romantic night inside with Nicole to make up for being gone all weekend.

Once he arrived home, he opened the door to his apartment and found Nicole sitting on the couch, bundled up in a blanket watching Lifetime. It was always some crazy shit playing on that channel, and Nicole loved every bit of it. Derek never understood what was so great about watching the same movie over and over again, but with different actresses.

"Honey, I'm home," he yelled out jokingly with his arms spread wide as if he was waiting for her to run into them.

"About time," Nicole responded with an attitude still looking at the TV.

Placing the groceries down on the counter, Derek walked over to Nicole with the flowers and chocolates he bought her in hand.

"For you," he said, standing in front of her.

"Move, you're in my way," Nicole responded, moving him to the side without paying any attention to his kind gesture.

"You're rude as fuck," Derek said, slamming her flowers down on the coffee table, sending the petals flying.

"The only reason you're giving me that shit is because you don't want to hear me bitching about you being gone all weekend, and today is your lucky day because I don't feel like hearing your sorry-ass excuse for *why* you've been gone." She was fed up. "Now, let me watch my movie." Grabbing the chocolate from him, she turned back towards the television.

"What you mean 'sorry-ass excuse'?" he asked as if he was offended, but he knew exactly what she meant.

"Weren't you supposed to be helping a friend move, and that was it? But somehow…you ended up gone an extra day because of 'work,'" she continued, as she made quotation marks with her fingers.

"Man, what do I need to do for you to get rid of this stank-ass attitude?" he asked, pulling her close and kissing her cheek.

"Oh, no, baby, that slick shit ain't working tonight. But what you can do is come with me to my sister's baby shower on Saturday. That might do it," she said, patting him on the chest.

"Ain't that shit for women?" He was already looking for a way out.

"Nope, it's co-ed, and if you don't want to sleep on the couch for the week, I'd suggest you say 'yes.'"

"For you," he said, kissing her on the cheek again and getting off the couch.

Walking into the kitchen, he poured himself a glass of wine, put the popcorn in the microwave, and everything else in the fridge. He had no use for the strawberries and whipped cream tonight.

I don't want to go to this fucking baby shower, he thought, placing both hands on the counter before walking back over to Nicole.

I know his cheating ass don't want to go…

Chapter Twenty-Three
Rebecca & Brandon

"The tension between you and your brother is more awkward than the encounter I had with Regina's sister," Rebecca said, as she placed dishes in the sink.

"Since you brought it up…I'm supposed to be going to meet Nasir with Gary after work tomorrow," he said, closing the trash bags to take them outside. "How do you feel about it?"

"You two were friends *way* before I came into the picture, so if you're comfortable going to speak to him, that's okay with me," she shrugged. "My feelings for him are long gone, so there shouldn't be any reason why everyone can't be adults and go on with life."

"You right. I'm just hoping this shit goes smooth because we both know how he can be," he said, shaking his head.

Don't I know it!

Nasir always had to have it his way, and he never felt like he was in the wrong. It may have been the one thing she didn't like about him when they were together.

"I guess that means we'll be going to that baby shower then," she laughed, as she

100

kissed him on the cheek and headed upstairs to get ready for bed.

"I guess so…I'll be up there in a minute."

When did I become the woman who gets in-between friends? Rebecca thought as she began to undress. She still felt somewhat bad about being the reason they weren't as close as they used to be. Maybe, if they got cool again, things wouldn't be so weird between him and Gary.

Rebecca ran herself a bubble bath and set up her tripod in the bathroom. She wanted to record a quick vlog recapping the movie night they had. Her subscribers were becoming increasingly interested in her day-to-day, so she figured *why not?* Plus, giving her audience Rev Run bathtub vibes would bring in the views, which brought in those extra coins she was growing accustomed to.

Grabbing her glass of wine, she placed it on the rim of the tub, grabbed her clicker for the camera, and slipped into the bath.

"Wassup, y'all! Welcome to another episode of *Rebecca Loves a Read*. You all asked me to get a little more personal and give you a look into my day-to-day life, so here I am in my big ass tub with my glass of wine, giving you a playback of my day."

As Rebecca was about to continue talking, Brandon came walking into the bathroom butt-ass-naked.

"Woman, what you in here doing?" he asked, looking right into her camera. "You trying to make a porno?"

Brandon started doing a little dance in front of the camera until he heard Rebecca say, "Everyone, meet my fine-ass boyfriend Brandon."

He jumped in the bathtub so fast it sent Rebecca into the biggest outburst of laughter.

"Don't worry, babe, I'll cover up that beautiful blessing between your legs," she said, kissing him on the lips.

"Why cover it up? Let your fans see what got you hooked on me," he said, seductively.

"…anyway, babe, I was getting my Rev Run on and letting them know about the amazing movie night we had; *nothing* but classic black films…"

Rebecca and Brandon filmed for almost an hour. Brandon wasn't supposed to ever appear in any of her videos. She didn't want to become one of those YouTube couples you see posted all over social media, but the way they were vibing so naturally, she knew her subscribers would love it and would want to see more of him. To her surprise, Brandon also enjoyed being in front of the camera. He was so used to making magic behind the scenes that he had no clue what it felt like being the center of attention.

"I have to admit…that was fun," he said, slipping into the bed next to Rebecca. "When are you going to upload it?"

"Probably sometime tomorrow. I still need to edit all that good dick out of my footage."

"You want some of this good dick in you?" he asked, rolling over onto Rebecca.

"Stop playing," she giggled.

"I'm dead-ass serious." He slid his hand up her shirt to rub on her thighs.

Gosh, he knows that gets me every time, she thought to herself, as she reached over to place her phone down on the nightstand.

Letting Brandon know it was a go, she began pulling her boy shorts off as he sucked on her neck.

"I knew you wanted this dick," he laughed, as Rebecca began to pull his briefs down.

"So, shut up and give it to me then," she said, wrapping her legs around his waist to pull him in.

Damn, Brandon thought, as he slid smoothly into Rebecca. He loved how well they fit together—inside and outside the bedroom.

Giving her slow, deep strokes and passionate kisses, he looked into her eyes and said, "I love you."

"I love you too," she said, using all her force to roll over on top of him.

Pulling her shirt over her head, Brandon began to massage her beautiful breasts as she grinded her hips back and forth on his dick.

Pulling her into him, Brandon continued to kiss Rebecca as she kissed his dick with her pussy. They were making love, and he was enjoying every minute of it.

Rebecca began to pick up the pace, and Brandon could feel her love coming down, sending him into overdrive. As she moaned out his name, he came inside her.

Once he was done, she placed a kiss on his lips and lay on his chest, as they fell fast asleep.

Chapter Twenty-Four
Nasir & The Boys

Looking at his Rolex, Nasir sat at the bar waiting for Gary and Brandon to show up so they could be seated. He requested a booth towards the back of the restaurant just in case the conversation went completely left. He knew he should've been fine with Rebecca moving on, but seeing that it was with someone he looked at as a brother had him fucked up in the head.

Before going to work that morning, Nasir let Ashley know that he would be home a little late because he was having a meeting with the boys, and, of course, she wasn't thrilled about it. The reason he was having this get-together anyway was partially her fault. No one told her to invite Brandon and Rebecca to the baby shower, but the petty part of her couldn't resist. She didn't think the two of them would say, "yes." Just when she thought she got rid of one brother, here came Gary trying to play peacemaker.

Getting anxious, Nasir ordered a double shot of Hennessy and headed to his table.

"...if you see a set of twins, can you direct them to the booth in the back?" he asked the hostess.

"Of course…can I get you started with anything while you wait?" she kindly asked.

"Bring two rounds of Hennessy shots and two orders of buffalo wings," he said, pulling out his phone to check in with Ashley.

"Hey, babe!"

"Hey," she said, sounding half asleep.

"Just wanted to see how you were doing. I know you don't like being home by yourself at night."

"I'm okay. I'm getting ready for bed. I'm exhausted."

"All right. Well, I'm still waiting on the twins, but I should be home in a few hours."

"Sounds good. Love you," Ashley said, before hanging up.

"Love you too."

Just as Nasir hung up the phone, Brandon and Gary were coming his way. Brandon already looked like he had an attitude, but Nasir decided to keep his cool for Gary's sake.

"Your guests are here, and your drinks will be out shortly. Let me know if you guys need anything else."

"Wassup, bruh?" Gary said, sliding into the booth with Brandon following behind, making sure to sit in the middle.

Gary wanted to keep as much space as he could between the two of them just in case they found themselves unable to control their hands. Hopefully, things didn't go that far, but Gary wasn't chancing it.

106

"So, y'all just gonna act like you don't see each other?" Gary asked, looking at Nasir and then back at Brandon.

Thank goodness, Brandon thought, as the waiter approached the table with their food and drinks. He immediately grabbed two shots and took them both back, but it didn't make him feel any better. No amount of alcohol would ease the tension between them.

"What's good?" he said, nodding his head at Nasir. "I'm here, so let's not start with the small talk. Get whatever you have to say off your chest and if at the end of this, we're not friends, I'm coo with it."

All Nasir could do was shake his head. The way Brandon came at him had him feeling a way.

"I see you not holding nothing back, so I'm not about to either," he said, taking his shot back next. "You had me fucked up."

"I don't see what the problem is." Brandon clasped his hands together and placed them on the table.

"Is he serious, or he got jokes?" Nasir looked at Gary confused as fuck.

"I'm dead serious, bruh. Don't you got a baby coming? So, what's the issue?"

"The issue is you started fuckin' my bitch..."

"She ain't no bitch." Brandon cut off Nasir before he could even finish. "And you not gon' start disrespecting her just because she decided where she was supposed to be was with me."

107

"Man," Gary said, shaking his head, "we not about to be doing this back-and-forth shit. Let Nasir get what he needs to get off his chest, so we can dead this shit and get back to how we used to be."

"All I need this nigga to do is admit that he was wrong as fuck for moving in on my chick before I was even done with her," Nasir said, taking his second shot.

Gary grabbed a plate of wings and leaned back into the booth.

"Well, B..."

"All right, I'll admit I was wrong for moving in on Rebecca as quick as I did, but I'm not about to say 'sorry' because I'm in love with her, bro, and she's who I plan on spending my life with."

"And you expect me to be cool with that?"

"You ain't got to be cool with nothing, but if we're going to move forward like the *brothers* we say we are, you need to respect it. You made your choice when you fucked around with Ashley, and Rebecca chose to be with me."

"So, it's like that? You just gon' keep fucking with her even though I'm not cool with it?" Nasir asked, already knowing it would be a long shot trying to get Brandon to break things off with her.

"Yeah, it's like that. It's not like I've just been dealing with her for a few months. We're getting real serious, so as far as you wanting us to stop what we're doing, it's not happening." Brandon grabbed some wings and called the waitress over for another shot.

"Sounds like y'all got this all figured out, so what shall we wear to the baby shower?" Gary asked, trying to get rid of the tension in the room.

"You sure you even want me and Rebecca there?"

"It would be rude not to come since y'all already RSVP'd," Nasir responded, wishing Ashley hadn't sent that invitation.

Nasir hadn't seen Rebecca since that day at Taste when she caught him tonguing down Ashley. How would he even react to seeing her face-to-face? How would she react? The idea of being able to be in her presence again excited him, but it would also be a reminder that she was no longer his...or, maybe, it would make her realize that she wanted to give it another chance.

"Aye, Kim," Gary yelled across the restaurant to a petite woman who stood at 5'2 with a brunette bob. She was wearing a black pencil skirt, a polka dot blouse, and red bottoms.

As she turned around, Nasir immediately put his head down, trying to hide his face.

"Nasir, it's another one of your old flames," he laughed, as he waved her over.

"How is it that we always run into someone from the past while we're here?"

"You shouldn't have done that," Brandon said, looking over at Nasir.

Excited to see Gary's face, Kim strolled over to the table, but the sight of Nasir sent her into a panic attack. Gary could see that something wasn't right, and the sweat dripping from Nasir's head only confirmed his suspicions.

"Y'all good?" he asked, as he stood up to greet Kim.

"I-I-I gotta go," she mumbled, before running towards the front, knocking over a tray on her way out.

"...that was weird," Gary said, sitting back down.

If only you knew, Brandon thought to himself.

Chapter Twenty-Five
Gary

After running into Kim, Brandon, and Nasir immediately said their "goodbyes" and headed home to their women. Gary didn't have shit else to do, so he decided to hang back and have a few more drinks at the bar. The way Kim ran out of the restaurant still had him confused. She looked so happy to be running into a few old college friends before she saw Nasir. The two of them used to be inseparable, kind of like him and Ashley. She even favored her.

One day, she just stopped coming around and was nowhere to be found on campus. Rumor was that she had lost her scholarship and had to drop out, but Nasir randomly stopped mentioning her name completely. Gary thought it was a little weird, but he wasn't that pressed to find out what happened. Whatever went on between them though, he was determined to find out what it was.

"What are you doing out so late?" Gary heard a woman's voice ask but didn't bother turning around to see who it was.

Sitting down next to him, the woman grabbed his drink to get his attention.

111

I *know this bitch didn't just snatch my drink*, he thought, as he turned around to see Shantel.

"You know you buying me another drink, right?" he said, shaking his head and waving the bartender over.

"Another Hennessy on the rocks?" a tall slender Caucasian man asked.

"Make that two," Shantel added, scooting herself closer to Gary and placing her hand on his inner thigh.

Oh, this bitch is crazy, he thought, as he pushed her hand away. She hadn't changed, and she felt no remorse for trying to push up on her sister's man. If this was a year ago and Brandon hadn't already fucked her, Gary would've been all over her, especially with them little-ass clothes she liked wearing, but he wasn't stupid. He knew that she had an argument with Regina for saying some slick shit, and Shantel would've loved to run back to Regina to throw some bullshit in her face.

"Why you acting funny?" she asked, placing her hand back on his thigh.

"You real bold, huh? Didn't Regina just smack the shit out of you a couple of days ago? You might wanna back yo' hoe-ass up."

"I got something else I can back up," she replied, rubbing her hand across his dick. "*And*, it's hard," she smiled.

"Oh, you real disrespectful," Gary said, getting up to leave the bar.

That bitch had him feeling a little horny, and he had to go before he did something that he was going to regret.

"Tell my sister I said, 'hi.'"

Shantel blew him a kiss goodbye and watched him walk out the door in a hurry.

Mission accomplished, she thought to herself, as she sat down and drank the two drinks they ordered. *Bet that bitch won't try me again.*

Gary hopped in his car feeling violated as ever.

Is this how I was making bitches feel?

Wondering if he should call and let Regina know what was up, he decided against it. Instead, he pulled out his phone to call his brother; Brandon would know the best way to deal with the situation.

"You won't believe who showed up at the bar when y'all left."

"Who?" Brandon's voice echoed throughout the car.

"Hey, Gary." He could hear Rebecca in the back.

"Tell her I said, 'wassup?' But Shantel's crazy-ass, and she was trying to push up on me *extra* hard."

"There is something wrong with that girl," Brandon responded, shaking his head. "You better tell Regina immediately."

"You think?" Gary asked as he pulled into his driveway.

"I *know*. You see what she did to Nasir."

"Man, you right." He turned off his car and leaned his seat back.

For a moment, he almost forgot about the video she sent to Rebecca. For all he knew, she could have been plotting on him as well.

"I'm a call Gina as soon as I get in the house. Before I hang up though," he said, sitting back up, "Why was Nasir acting so weird with Kim? They were both acting kind of funny, to be honest."

"I can't even get into that with you, bro. That's something he needs to tell you."

"Whole time you've been mad at me, but it sounds like you niggas got some secrets of your own…it's good. I'll find out what it is soon."

"Just know it ain't good," Brandon said, before hanging up the phone.

Gary walked into the house ready to crash. It was going on midnight, and he had a full day of filming ahead of him. He was doing everything he could to keep on schedule so investors wouldn't back out last minute. There was no way that he and Brandon would be able to pay all that money back if things didn't fall through.

Turning on the shower, Gary shot Regina a quick text and then sat his phone down. She was still super busy with work, being that she had taken over a lot of Ashley's things, so he didn't want to wake her up with a phone call.

Gary:
Baby, when you wake up in the morning, call me. I need to talk to you about your sister and some hoe-ass shit she tried to pull tonight. She's going overboard…anyway, love you and goodnight.

114

Chapter Twenty-Six

Kim

Stumbling to her car, Kim began to have flashbacks of the night that left her with a scar underneath her right eye and a crooked index finger.

She fumbled with her keys as she struggled to unlock the door; her hands were sweaty and shaking.

"Are you all right, sweetie?" an older black woman asked, as she watched Kim drop her keys on the ground.

"...I'm just fine," her voice scratched.

"You don't seem like it." The woman came closer to try and help.

"Don't touch me!" she said, shoving the woman away. "I'm fine."

"If you say so, child."

The woman turned to walk away before she took one last glance. Kim looked like a woman running away from a ghost, in shock and terrified. For Kim, that's exactly what it was, a ghost from her past that she thought she had left behind. It took years of therapy to get over what Nasir had done to her in that dorm room. Kim no longer knew how to trust men, afraid that one wrong word or one too many drinks would lead to her being in a hospital bed for weeks.

116

Kim went on to have a daughter, but, even then, she couldn't hold onto the relationship she had with the father because she was stuck holding onto what had happened to her. All he wanted to do was love her and build a life they could both be proud of, but Kim was too busy trying to find something wrong with him and their relationship. The uncertainty and lack of trust sent her daughter's father running the other way.

"Relax. Everything is going to be okay," she reassured herself, as she sat in her car with tears rolling down her face.

"1-2-3-4," Kim began to count. "He is the past. He can no longer hurt me. I am stronger than my scars."

Those were the words she repeated to herself when she felt like the walls were closing in on her.

I am stronger than my scars.

Nasir Wright would not be the reason she backslid into depression. Kim was on the right track and had connected with her family again. The only reason she decided to leave Miami was to be close to her little sister, who had just graduated. Her mother had also made the move to be closer to her baby girl.

Kim found a job at an advertising company as a financial adviser which she loved, and she met a handsome young man who made her feel like royalty. There was no way she was running away. It was time to finally face her past.

The sound of her cell phone ringing let her escape her thoughts just for a moment; it was her boyfriend.

"Everything okay?" Kim panicked.

"Nothing I can't handle. Ari had a nightmare and wanted to talk to you before she went back to sleep."

"Put her on the phone."

"...Mommy, the bad lady was trying to take me away," Kim's 4-year-old whined into the phone.

"Mommy will never let anyone take you away, okay? I promise. And, plus, you have Nick there to keep you safe."

"Yeah, he's pretty great," she said, looking over at Nick.

"Mommy will be there soon. I love you."

"Love you too," she responded, before handing the phone back to Nick.

"Thank you, babe."

"You good?"

"I'll be better once I'm next to you...be home in a little bit. Thank you for being so good to us," she said before she hung up.

Chapter Twenty-Seven
Nikki & Rebecca

Nikki sat at the silver vanity in the studio doing her makeup. The bags underneath her eyes showed the lack of sleep she received, but her cheeks still had a rosy glow to them that left her looking like a teenage girl in love.

"I can't believe you have me out of bed this early," she said to Rebecca, while still looking at herself in the mirror.

It was 5 a.m., and they were getting ready to record their podcast, but this time they were also filming, which meant Nikki needed to make herself up. The topic for the day was *Is It Too Soon to Move-In with Your Boo?* Monica finally had the guts to mention moving in with Nikki a few days ago, and it led to an argument. Ever since that fight, Monica hadn't been coming over to Nikki's house, and she wasn't speaking to her much either. The stress of not knowing what was going to happen between the two of them was eating away at her, and she was starting to wonder if Monica was just going to say fuck her and run into the arms of a man like her ex had.

Nikki was still trying to figure out where the question even came from.

119

Monica had come over after a long day of filming. They went to dinner and a movie, then went back to Nikki's to relax. In the middle of their making love, Monica asked if they could move in together. Nikki didn't have a response, so she kept sucking the life out of Monica's juice box, hoping it was just something she was saying because Nikki was making her orgasm like crazy. It wasn't until Monica pushed her head away and sat up that she realized she was serious, and from there, everything went left.

"You should have been wide awake anyway. Didn't Monica have to be on set early?"

"She didn't stay over last night, so I was on my own this morning," she responded as if everything was okay.

"You ready to get this shit going?" Rebecca asked, walking over to the pink sofa sitting in front of a pink wall, with a huge portrait of Sade in the background, and a white marble coffee table in front. A gold and white chandelier hung from the ceiling, and white roses sat on the side tables next to the couch.

The space Brandon picked out was perfect, but it was Rebecca's touch that made it *pop*. When Nikki and Rebecca decided to find a space to record their podcast, she also knew it would be good for her vlog as well. Rebecca had a vision and wanted her audience to feel like they were right there with them.

"You know my saying," Nikki said, getting up.

"As ready as I'ma get," they said in unison.

Sitting on the couch, Nikki took a sip of her venti caramel frap with two shots of espresso, took one last look at her phone to see if Monica had texted her, and then put it on silent.

"Let's go," she said, looking at Rebecca.

"Hey, everyone! Welcome to another episode of *Double the Fun* with your favorite ladies Rebecca and Nikki Shay. How are you this morning, Nikki?"

"Tired as hell," she admitted, taking a sip of her drink.

"Well, you don't look it," Rebecca smiled. "Today's episode will be posted on our YouTube channel, so you'll be able to see how fine Miss Nikki Shay looks, y'all."

"You guys see how she's always trying to make me blush? But anyway, tell the people what we'll be discussing today."

"Moving in with your significant other," Rebecca responded, excitedly. "I've finally done it, but I want to go more into when is the right time. Is it ever too soon? Right now, I'm living with my boyfriend, and it took about six months before I decided to stay permanently," she continued, "but I dated a man for years, and we never made it to that step."

"What stopped you the first time? Three years is a long time."

"Honestly, I didn't feel the need to. We spent so much time in each other's space that it was nice being able to go home and not have to fight over someone taking up all the space in the bed or using all the hot water," Rebecca laughed.

"Well, I've for sure done the whole *living with your significant other* thing in the past, and now I'm not sure how I feel about making that move again."

"Why not, girl? I love having dick on demand. Sitting there all long, thick, and handsome, just waiting for me to sit on it." Rebecca licked her lips and rolled her hips.

"Bitch, you being nasty this early in the morning?" Nikki laughed. "You definitely had some dick before you got here."

"…maybe, but you still didn't answer the question."

"I've lived with an ex in the past, and we all know how that turned out. She put me out and for a man at that, which reminds me that if anything were to ever go wrong, there's a chance that one of us could be left with no place to go," Nikki said, in all seriousness.

"That's the one reason I decided to rent out my place. I have faith in my relationship, but in case anything should happen, I know I could always go back to the home I created before him."

"I wish I was that smart back then," Nikki said, shaking her head, and feeling a little embarrassed.

"How soon did you move in with your ex?" Rebecca was curious to know.

"You know how us lesbians move," Nikki laughed. "By the third date, we were making plans to move in with each other, and two months into dating, we had a spot. We weren't even officially together yet," she smiled, as she reminisced on what was.

About a little over an hour later, they had finally finished recording. They had gotten so caught up in the conversation that they forgot about the time limits they had set for themselves, but they covered some good ground and knew more than a few people would appreciate the different views about moving in and how soon. Nikki was just happy that Rebecca didn't ask about her and Monica.

"That was a good episode," Rebecca said, cleaning up the space.

"It was. Glad I picked it."

"Why did you pick it? Are you thinking about moving with Mo?"

Welp, I spoke too soon, Nikki thought to herself before answering.

"...as much as I would love to, and as much as I love her, I can't do it...and now, she's pissed off about it."

"Did you tell her why?"

"No, but you know about my ex, and being that it was only a year ago that she was messing with Gary's hoe-ass, and who knows who else, I can't take that chance again,"

Nikki said, grabbing her purse hoping to end the conversation.

"She's my friend and all, but I know where you're coming from. You two just need to sit down like adults and have a real conversation about why you're hesitant. I know how Mo can be, but I think she really likes you. I've never known her to want to move in with someone before," Rebecca said, hugging Nikki before letting her go. "Let me know how it goes."

"You'll be the first to know," she said, closing the door behind her.

Chapter Twenty-Eight
Regina

The sun had yet to rise, and the sky still looked as dark as night. The alarm was yelling out to Regina, but she kept trying to silence it like a mother does a toddler in a crowded restaurant. After going off for the fifth time, she managed to roll out of the bed with her eyes slightly opened. It was 5 in the morning, but Regina got herself into a routine of waking up a few hours early to get some self-care in.

Rubbing the sleep out of her eyes, she walked over to her tub to run herself a bubble bath. As the water ran, she walked to the kitchen to boil some water for tea. Since Ashley went on leave, Regina no longer had a personal barista to bring her a cup of coffee to work, so tea became her morning go-to.

Walking into the kitchen, Regina tried to be as silent as she could be. Shantel was on the couch snoring like a bear, and she didn't want to wake her; although the minute the kettle started to whistle, she'd be up with an attitude as always, but Regina didn't care. Shantel came banging on her door at 2 in the morning, drunk as hell, saying something about losing her keys, but Regina was too tired to ask any questions. She just opened the door and threw Shantel a blanket and a pillow before rushing back to bed.

Running back to her room to turn off the bath before it ran over, she finally checked her phone and saw a message from Gary. The minute she saw Shantel's name, she wanted to flip, knowing the two of them and how they behaved in the past.

After walking over to the door to close it, she dialed up Gary.

"...what you mean my sister was doing some hoe-shit?" she asked, as soon as Gary said, "hello".

"Well, good morning to you too," he responded, still sounding half-sleep.

"Good morning," Regina said, rolling her eyes. "Why were you with my sister last night?"

"Before you jump to conclusions," Gary said, sitting up in his bed, "I wasn't with your sister. I stayed behind at the bar when Nas and Brandon left, and she happened to end up there."

"Well, what happened? Because her drunk-ass is over here on my couch right now."

"After the guys left, I stayed behind to have a few more drinks, and long story short, your sister started to get touchy-feely, trying to rub on my dick and shit. So, I got my ass up out of there before I had to get disrespectful."

"Babe, let me call you back," Regina responded, hanging up the phone before Gary could say anything else.

Swinging her door wide open, Regina went storming into the living room like a bat out of hell. The kettle going off only added extra commotion to the whole situation. Shantel could hear all the noise, but she turned to face the back of the couch like she didn't.

"Get the fuck up!" Regina snatched Shantel off the couch and onto the floor.

Oh, this bitch is trippin', Shantel thought, as she struggled to open her eyes. They felt heavy as hell, her head was pounding, the room looked like it was spinning, and the feeling of alcohol sitting in her throat was making her want to vomit. As much as she wanted to get up and defend herself, she just didn't have the strength to be arguing before the sun rose.

"You just don't know when to quit, do you? You need to get out of my house now," Regina said, leaning down to help Shantel get off the ground.

"I got it," she said, snatching her arm away. "I don't even know what the fuck you're talking about this damn early in the morning."

"So, you don't remember putting those nasty-ass hands of yours on my man last night?"

"Well, look at that...he called and told you. I bet he didn't tell you that he liked it

127

though," Shantel smirked. "One more drink and he would've been ready to dive into my ocean."

"Bitch, I should slap yo' punk-ass right now. I see why David never liked you."

"David didn't like me, because he couldn't fuck me, and trust me...he tried."

Before Shantel could grab her belongings, Regina had her by the hair, dragging her out the door kicking and screaming like the drama queen she was.

Walking back into the house, Regina grabbed her sister's purse and shoes and threw those out the door too.

"I hope you know not to ever come back around here again. I'm done with you and the drama that comes with it. You're an evil miserable bitch," Regina yelled before slamming the door behind her, leaving Shantel on the ground looking sick.

How dare she bring up David? Regina thought as she walked into the kitchen to turn off the screaming kettle. It was like Shantel was looking to get a reaction out of her.

Regina knew her sister was up to no good, but she had no clue that she'd come for her like that. This was the second time within a few days that she had to lay hands on Shantel for bringing up the men in her life. David was the man she was supposed to spend forever with, and Shantel thought it was okay to speak on his name and then throw out some bullshit allegation about him

128

trying to sleep with her, knowing that he wasn't around to defend himself. Then, she was coming for Gary's character once again, trying to prove that he wasn't capable of being a faithful man. Regina was over it, and as much as it was going to hurt to have to cut her sister out of her life, she was starting to believe that it needed to be done because she was never going to stop.

Pouring herself a cup of tea, Regina needed to reset, and work was no longer on her schedule. Grabbing her work bag off of the dining room chair, she headed back into her room and plopped down on the bed. Sitting her cup on the nightstand, she pulled out her laptop to email her boss.

Good morning, Ronda,

Sorry for the short notice, but I will not be able to come into the office today, due to food poisoning. I will do some phone follow-ups when my body allows and do my best to make it back into the office tomorrow morning. Again, sorry for the late notice.

Best regards,
Regina Thomas

Chapter Twenty-Nine
Shantel

S hantel rarely felt bad for the shit she did to people, but the way she and Regina ended that argument wasn't sitting right with her. She knew bringing up David was going to strike a nerve in Regina, and that's exactly why she did. In all honesty, Shantel wished that David would have approached her, instead of Regina. From the moment he stepped into their lives, Shantel had a crush on him and was envious of the relationship they had. David gave Regina whatever she wanted and praised the ground she walked on. Meanwhile, Shantel had to use her body to stay relevant to the men she brought around.

When David passed away, Shantel finally felt like she could catch up with Regina, maybe even surpass her in life, but somehow, Regina always came out on top, leaving Shantel to look like the evil dumb little sister.

"Where did I even park?"

Shantel stood on the side of the curb, rubbing the back of her head. It felt like Regina pulled out a chunk of her hair when she snatched her up, or maybe, it was the pounding headache she had from the shots of Hennessy she continued to take after Gary left the bar.

Going into her purse, she fumbled around for her keys, only to realize she didn't even drive once she looked at her phone. There was a text from her friend, asking if the Uber driver got her home safely.

Why did I even come over here? she thought, rubbing her head again.

Sitting down on the curb and waiting for her Uber to come, she tried to remember why she came to her sister's house in the first place. Going back into her phone and looking through her pictures, she saw what she was coming to show Regina—a picture of her and Gary looking cozy.

I must've been too drunk to show her these, she thought. *Too late now, she's going to believe him before she does me.*

Getting the notification that her ride was approaching, Shantel stood up and immediately puked on the curb.

"You good, lil' mama? I don't need you throwing up in my car," the driver said, stopping in front of her.

"Just get me home please," she said, opening the door.

Once inside, she rested across the backseat and closed her eyes...drifting off once again.

Chapter Thirty
Gary

When Regina didn't call him back immediately, Gary figured Shantel was over there telling lies about what went down, but about two hours later, he finally got that callback, asking him to come over. He should've been heading to the studio to get some filming done, but he knew Brandon could handle shit on his own nowadays. There was no way he was going to keep his woman at the house crying over some stupid shit her sister did.

Regina swore she was okay, but Gary had been with her long enough to recognize when something was wrong. He could hear the sadness and anger in her voice, and the fact that she called off from work, which was usually *never*, told him all he needed to know.

Jumping in his car, he made his way to the store before heading over to Regina's house. He couldn't think of a better way of spending his day.

Once he finished picking up a few things, he pulled into the parking lot of her complex. After parking in his usual spot, he grabbed the bag of body oils and food he had sitting in the passenger seat and made his way up to her place.

132

"...you didn't have to do that," Regina said happily, as she looked at the bag in Gary's hand.

"But I did," he responded, walking through the door. "I'm going to cook you breakfast, run you a bath, and then give you the best massage you've ever had."

"You're the best," Regina said, embracing Gary.

Feeling his arms around her made her forget about the morning she was having. Gary had become her safe place, and that's the way she wanted to keep it. If it meant losing out on a relationship with her sister, she was perfectly okay with that. Her dad wouldn't be happy...but, *oh, well.* Regina thought she'd never find a man who could make her feel remotely close to the feeling David had given her, but Gary was proving her wrong. Everything people painted him out to be was nothing close to what she had experienced in their time together.

"Go relax."

Gary kissed Regina on the lips and made his way into the kitchen. Making his way around the kitchen as if he were in his own home, he opened the bottom cabinet next to the stove and pulled out her stainless-steel frying pans; then, he grabbed a mixing bowl and began whipping up his famous infusion. Regina loved the mixture of soy sauce, lemon juice, and hot pepper sauce together, amongst the many other ingredients he refused to reveal.

Spreading the mixture over his meat, he let it sit as he began to cut up red potatoes.

While Regina caught up on episodes of *Grey's Anatomy*, Gary watched as she tried to sneak glimpses of him making his special sauce.

"Mind yo' business, woman," he said, pretending to cover up his food.

"*You* are my business," she smirked, then turned back towards the TV.

"Yeah, yeah."

An hour later, Gary was done cooking. He plated her food like the professional chef he once thought of becoming, before bringing it over to her on a tray. He could see Regina was into her episode, and he didn't want to interrupt her.

"Aren't you going to eat?"

"Nah, you enjoy," he said, kissing her on the forehead. "I'm going to run you a bath."

Damn, I love that man.

Lining her jacuzzi tub and bedroom with candles, Gary turned on some Trey Songz to set the mood and waited for Regina to enter the room. For years, women begged and pleaded for him to give them this kind of treatment, but it wasn't his thing. He didn't know anything about being a gentleman, and quite frankly, he was still learning. But he liked who he was becoming; his mama would be proud.

There was something about Regina that brought out the best in him, and he knew she deserved the world. For once, he saw himself having a future with one woman, and he wasn't about to mess it up for *nothing*...or *no* one.

Walking into the room satisfied with the 5-star meal Gary had made her, Regina's eyes shined bright as she looked around her made-over room.

"This way, my lady," Gary said, grabbing her hand.

Standing in front of her tub, which was filled with an assortment of flowers, including lotuses, roses, and sweet jasmine, Gary undressed Regina slowly while placing kisses on her shoulders.

"It's time to relax," he whispered in her ear.

Stepping into the floral bath, one foot at a time, Gary admired her body. She slowly slid down into the water and closed her eyes. The smell of lavender filled the air, and instant relief came over her. She no longer felt anxious and stressed out.

Reaching towards her washcloth, Gary gently pushed her hand away.

"I got this."

Sitting on the edge of the tub, he began to wash Regina from head to toe, making her feel like the queen he knew she was. Her skin glistened as if she was covered in the finest gloss and felt smooth like butter.

Once he finished washing her body, he proceeded to wash her hair, almost putting her to sleep. Lifting Regina out of the tub, he walked her over to the bed, placing her on the towel he had laid out. Wiping her body down, he then grabbed the massage oil off the nightstand and poured a nice amount in his hands.

"What did I do to deserve this?" Regina asked as he dug his masculine hands into her thick thighs.

"Everything."

Turning over to face him, Gary poured oil over her flat stomach and thick thighs. Taking his hands, he massaged up to her perfect 36D breasts. As he watched her nipples get hard, Regina slightly spread her legs, inviting him inside. Straddling over her, Gary placed his hands between her thighs and began to rub them in a circular motion, moving up to her hips and stomach. As he brought his hands back down, they glided against her slick pussy, back down to her thighs. Noticing her body language, Gary knew it was time to give her clit some attention. With every stroke of his hand, Regina began to moan louder, and he could feel how moist she was becoming.

"Come here," she said, pulling at the neck of his shirt.

Pulling it over his head, Gary leaned down and began kissing Regina passionately, still massaging her pussy with one hand.

Reaching for his waist, she struggled to pull down his sweatpants. But, with a little assistance, she managed to get them over his muscular ass.

Flipping herself onto her stomach, she poked her butt up in the air a little.

"Slide in," she whispered, seductively.

Easing his dick into her warm pussy, Gary massaged her ass as he watched her pussy cover his dick in juices.

"I love the way you fuck me." Regina looked back.

"I know you do," he said, grabbing her by the neck and stuffing his tongue in her mouth, as he sped up his rhythm, causing Regina to squirt.

"Damn, girl," he smiled, as she began to throw it back.

With his last thrust, Gary grabbed onto her hips and let his love flow through her.

I think I'm in love, he thought, as he rested on her back.

Chapter Thirty-One
Nasir & Ashley

For days, Nasir tossed and turned in his sleep, thinking about Kim. Rebecca was no longer the woman consuming his thoughts anymore. His sleep had gotten so bad that Ashley began sleeping in the guest room in fear that he'd hurt her in his sleep. She was already in enough pain from baby Nasir making her ribs his favorite resting spot; now, she had to worry about accidentally getting a black eye in the middle of the night. If she didn't know any better, she would've thought he had PTSD or something.

She knew something was wrong with Nasir, but with their baby shower just a day away, she didn't want to dive into what had his mind in the horrible state it was in.

Nasir could tell that Ashley could sense that something was going on within him, but he couldn't look at her and say, "I saw my ex…who I put in the hospital." He didn't want her to look at him like she did every other man in her life—with fear in her eyes and hate in her heart. But to Ashley, Nasir had always been a knight in shining armor, even after all their years of being separated.

Even after he played her out like a whore and used her to get over Rebecca, there was still something in him that she loved to death, and he didn't know what it was.

"Hey, babe," Nasir said, walking towards the kitchen.

"No work today?"

"No, I didn't get the best sleep again last night, so I decided to stay home. Anything you need me to help you with?"

"Since you asked," she said, rubbing her stomach, "You can come over here and help my big-ass fill these little bottles with candy, and wrap up these rice crispy treats until Brittney gets here."

Ashley was sitting in the middle of the living room floor with her pregnancy pillow wrapped around her, surrounded by at least twenty mini bottles tied with blue ribbons and filled with Lemonheads, and treats decorated with the initials NJ resting in a basket. Her hair now laid past her earlobes, and her bangs almost covered her eyes. For the first time in her eight months of being pregnant, she finally let her hair do its own thing, but it was growing faster than she liked. Nasir loved it though. As much as he liked how she looked with short hair, he secretly wanted her to grow it back.

"Don't we have someone to do all that?"

"Yes, but I wanted to feel like I had some part in making this baby shower beautiful, so are you going to come help me or not?"

"I mean...I can, but what did I spend money hiring all those people for?"

"Never-fucking-mind. You always have to be so damn difficult. Brit will be here soon anyway."

Ashley hated when Nasir would ask if she needed anything and then somehow find a way to complain about it. The whole week she had been overly irritated with him, and she was ready to lose it, but it was something she was going to have to deal with after their baby dropped.

Just when she thought everything was going good, things changed. Maybe, it was the meeting he had with Brandon that had him acting different, but she didn't like it.

"Someone has an attitude this morning," he laughed.

"First of all, it's noon. Maybe, you should look at the clock like you've been looking at that damn Facebook page of yours," Ashley snapped. "Secondly, don't offer your assistance when it's obvious that you don't want to give it."

"I should've took my ass to work," Nasir mumbled under his breath, hoping Ashley wouldn't hear him.

"You still can. No one needs that fucking energy around here," she yelled out in frustration.

The baby must've sensed the tension in the air because he sent a sharp pain through her stomach causing her to double over. See-ing the pain rush over her, Nasir ran to

Ashley's side, afraid that something was wrong with his child.

Sitting down on the ground, he wrapped his arms around her and began caressing her stomach with one hand and massaging her hair with the other.

"Are you okay?"

"Can you leave, Nasir?"

"I'm sorry, baby," he said, kissing her neck.

"Seriously, Nasir, I need you to leave. I'd rather not be stressed the day before our baby shower, and right now, your voice is pissing me off." Ashley moved his hand from off her stomach. "Go take a run on the coast and come back with a clear mind. We have people to entertain tomorrow."

"You're right. I'm sorry, Ash," he said, getting up off the floor, wondering how he was going to fix things this time.

Chapter Thirty-Two
Rebecca

The day was almost over, and Rebecca couldn't wait to get out of the office. Unlike most days, today was a little different.

She breezed through her work within the first few hours, and it left some time for her to finish up a few chapters before the day ended. The more she wrote, the easier it became to tell a story, and she even found inspiration from the manuscripts she'd been reading.

Once again, Diane had left Rebecca in charge of the office while she ran off to be with her handsome lawyer boo. Rebecca was waiting for the day she came in with a huge rock on her finger and handed the company over to her.

Since Rebecca had a few errands to run, she was about to tell the rest of the team to call it a day as well, especially since they didn't have any heavy deadlines to meet.

Just as she was about to shut down her laptop and slip her black heels back on, there was a knock at the door.

"Come in."

"I think I have something you may want to see," Laura said, walking inside with her drawing tablet in hand.

The butterflies in Rebecca's stomach started going wild.

"...is that what I think it is?"

"The best damn book cover you'll ever see," Laura said, revealing the cover of her novel.

For the longest, Nikki and Rebecca debated what they wanted the cover to look like. They wanted it to be simple, yet meaningful. The cover needed to be a symbol of what they both went through—love, heartbreak, strength, and rebirth.

As Laura sat the tablet in front of Rebecca, she saw a tear come from her eyes, but it was filled with so much joy. The background was all-white, with a light pink heart in the middle, which was broken open. It was surrounded by yellow, lavender, and peach flowers with butterflies coming out of the crack in the heart as if they were escaping towards a new life.

"So...do you like it?" Laura asked, nervously.

"You annoy me, girl, but I *love* it! Diane did an excellent job picking you for this position," Rebecca said, getting up to hug her.

"I thought I'd never hear those words come from you."

"Why?"

"Let's be honest, you and I both know you weren't too fond of me when I got here.

You did all you could to ignore me whenever I tried speaking to you," Laura said, crossing her arms. "But it's okay because I knew I'd eventually grow on you."

"Whatever," Rebecca said, grabbing her purse. "I'm about to head out, and I think you should too."

"Is Diane going to be okay with that?" Laura asked.

"Do you see her anywhere?"

"No."

"Well, there goes your answer. Matter of fact...come to the mall with me. I need to get a drink and an outfit for this baby shower I'm going to."

"Maybe, next time. I'm meeting up with my sister for drinks and dinner."

"Okay, I'm going to hold you to that...and thanks again, Laura. See you Monday." Rebecca walked out of the office towards the elevator.

As the door opened, a woman who resembled Ashley walked right past her. It caused Rebecca to do a double take.

Crazy, she thought, as the woman approached Laura.

"That must be the sister," she said to herself, as she waved to Laura and the woman as the doors closed.

Looking to find a super cute jumpsuit or something of the sort, Rebecca made her way to one of her favorite boutiques. Monica planned to meet her there, and Rebecca was positive that it had everything to do with the podcast she and Nikki did a few days before. Nikki never got back to her about how the whole "moving-in" talk went, which had her thinking the conversation must've gone completely left, but Rebecca was praying for the best.

Walking into the boutique, she had no idea what she was looking for. She had never been to a baby shower before, let alone the baby shower of an ex. The whole situation was just awkward.

Part of her wanted to be real casual, in hopes of going unnoticed by all of Nasir's family. She could already see the looks and hear the whispers of everyone judging her for showing up with the soon-to-be dad's best friend.

The other part of Rebecca wanted to wear something that caught the eyes of everyone in the room. Who cared if it was Ashley's baby shower? She wanted Nasir to see what he was missing out on...after all, that was supposed to be *her* baby and *her* shower, but now she had to start over once again.

While Rebecca waited on Monica, who was late as usual, she picked out a few outfits and made her way into the fitting room.

"Let me know if you need anything in a distinct size or color," the sales associate said, as she placed her items in the room.

Rebecca had tried on three outfits, none of which seemed appropriate for a baby shower, and there was still no sign of Monica, which was unusual. Rebecca was used to her being late, but she always showed up for her best friend.

Pulling out her phone, Rebecca dialed up Mo, but she sent her straight to voicemail.

Oh, this bitch must be trippin' today.

Before leaving, Rebecca sent Nikki a message to see if she had heard from Monica before deciding to try on one more outfit. She'd been eyeing this navy-blue jumpsuit with white and yellow flowers printed on it ever since she entered the store but was afraid it would look cheap on her. To her surprise, it hugged every curve on her body exactly right and made her breasts look perky. Her waist was snatched, and the jumpsuit left a little mid-drift open for all to admire her flat stomach.

This is it, Rebecca thought, as she looked at herself from every angle.

"I need to send this pic to B., show him how thick I'm getting," she said to herself, as she picked up her phone. Just then, a call from Nikki came through.

"Hey, girl," Rebecca answered. "Have you seen Mo?"

"About that…I'm pretty sure she's ignoring us."

"What the fuck did I do? She knows we had plans today," Rebecca responded. If she knew Monica wasn't going to show up, she would have been in and out.

"You home?"

"I'll be there in about thirty-, maybe thirty-five minutes," Rebecca said, coming out of the jumpsuit to get dressed.

"Can I meet you there? I'll explain everything."

"Yeah and bring some wine…vodka if you'd like."

Walking out of the store to her car, Rebecca ran into the last person she wanted to see.

"…I see you still have that keychain I got you."

Nasir was standing in front of Rebecca with the biggest smile on his face.

You've got to be fucking kidding me.

Chapter Thirty-Three
Nasir

Whenever Nasir felt like he was taking steps in a positive direction within his relationship, it seemed like something or someone from his past was standing in front of him, trying to push him backward with all the force they could. First, it was Rebecca; then, it was his job. Ashley complained about the time it took away from her, despite the money he was bringing in. Now, he had to deal with running into ghosts from his past. The last thing he wanted was for his demons to be revealed to the rest of the world.

Nasir didn't know whether it was karma, the universe telling him he needed to work on himself, or both. Either way, he needed to figure things out and quickly. His son was arriving soon, and he needed to make sure that he had a clear mind, not just for himself but for Ashley too. He made a promise to Ashley to be there for her no matter what, and he was trying to do everything to uphold that, even if he wasn't 100% sure she was the woman for him. For his son, he would make sure they remained a family, but if he didn't get it together, it would only be a matter of time before she was out of his life and took their son right along with her.

Doing his best not to cause any further arguments with Ashley, he did what she said and left the house. Usually, he would go to the gym or for a run to clear his head, but instead, he treated himself to a two-hour movie and then lunch. That should've been enough time for Ashley to cool down after talking all her shit to Brittney like he knew she would.

His mom would be arriving at their home in a few hours. He was hoping that if she spent some time alone with Ashley, she could calm her down. In the case that didn't work, Nasir figured he make his way towards the Fashion District to purchase Ashley a few things.

"Hey, Mom," Nasir said, answering his phone on the first ring.

"How is my favorite son in the whole wide world doing?"

"Woman, I'm your only son, but I'm doing good. About to go to a jewelry store and maybe pick out some clothes for after Ashley has the baby."

"What did you do to that girl this time?" his mom asked, knowing her son all too well.

"Let's just say she wasn't feeling my attitude and kicked me out of the house for the day."

"As she should," his mom laughed.

"What happened to me being your favorite?"

"You can be my favorite and still be in the wrong, son."

His mother was his biggest, yet realest fan. She never sugarcoated a thing and was the same way with his father, which is probably why they held their marriage together for so long. His dad knew she didn't take any shit, and she'd check him quick when he got out of line.

"Anyway, I was calling to let you know I'm about to board my plane and that I love you."

"I love you too, Ma," he said, getting out of his car. "Remember that my driver is picking you up, so be sure to look for a sign with your name next to baggage claim."

"Boy, I tell you. Kids get some money and act like they can't do shit on their own," she said right before hanging up.

"Mama," Nasir yelled into the phone, surprised that she hung up in his face.

Man, that lady is crazy, he thought, as he walked into the jewelry store to find Ashley the perfect diamond.

When he first got out of the car, he was leaning towards getting her the big-ass rock she had posted on her vision board, but he didn't want to lead her on, thinking they were headed down the aisle. Eventually, that was the goal, but for now, he wasn't ready. The only thing on his mind was making it through tomorrow. Instead, he opted for a pair of diamond earrings to match the necklace he bought her.

After making his purchase, Nasir decided to head up the street to see if he could find some flowers. On the way, he stopped in Starbucks to get an iced coffee, then headed to the flower shop around the corner.

Walking into the shop, he immediately spotted a beautiful balloon flower, which had just bloomed. He paired the purple flower with orange calendulas.

Nasir felt accomplished after making his purchase and was just about ready to make his way back home to hopefully a happier Ashley, but as he walked down the street, a matte black BMW truck with a red interior caught his eye. Immediately something inside him told him that it was Rebecca.

Knowing he should have kept on walking, he decided against it and peeked into the store and spotted her at the register. The way her body curved in her black pants suit made him think of the mornings he'd sneak up behind her, and she'd let him hit it from the back before making her way out the door.

Wanting to say, "hi," he waited patiently for her to come out of the boutique.

Rebecca came walking towards the door like a fashion model. Not once did she look up as she dug inside her purse for her keys.

"I see you still have that keychain I got you," he smirked, as Rebecca looked at him uninterested in what he had to say.

"Well, it is *my* initial, so what did you expect?" she asked, walking towards her door. "I need to get home."

"Can we talk? It's been a while, but I know you're going to the baby shower tomorrow. You'll look good in whatever you bought," he said, grabbing her wrist.

Snatching her arm away, Rebecca did the best she could to keep her composure.

"The only person you should be focusing on tomorrow is your woman," she said, opening her car door. "I'm only going to support Brandon and your friendship. Despite everything that's happened between the three of us, he loves you like a brother, and I'm not going to get in the way of that…and neither should you."

Nasir knew Rebecca was right, but he needed to know one last thing before he let her drive away.

"Do you ever think *what if?*"

"The what-ifs no longer matter, Nasir…now, have a good day. I'll see you at the baby shower," Rebecca said, closing the door and driving away, leaving Nasir in his thoughts.

They matter to me…

Chapter Thirty-Four
Rebecca

Driving away, Rebecca couldn't help but watch as Nasir faded in her rearview mirror. He looked so sad and lost, not like a man that was about to celebrate the life he'd always wanted. He had everything right in front of him, but it seemed like he was ready to risk it all just to try again.

Rebecca contemplated what he had said. It was her chance to get the closure she so desperately needed, but what was the point of looking back? They were over, and they both needed to let it be. There was no way she was going to do to Brandon what Nasir had done to her, but she still couldn't help but wonder...*what if he never told her they should've been friends—if she never found out about Ashley?*

Listening to Jhene Aiko's *Souled Out* album, Rebecca found herself in an alternate universe, one where she and Nasir were still together. The twins didn't exist, there was no Ashley around trying to insert herself into the picture, and everything was as perfect as she had always imagined. They had the fairytale wedding, they traveled the world for two years straight, and then finally settled in

New York after she found out that she was pregnant. They ended up having four children and lived in a $5.5 million home. Together, they were dominating the industries they worked in, and no one could knock them off their thrones. It was everything Rebecca had ever dreamed of, but she was knocked back into reality by the sounds of horns and angry drivers yelling obscenities at her.

"I'm going. I'm going...my goodness, calm your fucking nerves," she yelled out as if the people behind her could hear her through her rolled-up windows.

Rebecca was so caught up in her thoughts that she hadn't realized she had let two green lights pass her by.

I need to get it together before tomorrow, she thought, as she made her way home. Nikki Shay was probably already about to pull up to her house, and she still hadn't heard from Monica.

Pulling out her phone, she decided to give Nikki a call to let her know that she was running a bit behind.

"Hey, Nikki," she said, as she heard her voice pop up on the Bluetooth. "How far away are you from the house?"

"I should be there in about ten minutes. You good?"

"Besides running into Nasir...uh...I'm not sure. He threw me off, which is why I was calling to let you know I'll be a little bit behind you."

"Should I stop to grab anything? Like a bottle of tequila…?"

"No, Brandon has plenty to drink behind that little bar of his. He should be home, so once you get there, just let yourself in. I'll tell him you're on the way."

"All right, I'll see you soon…wait, have you heard from Monica yet? She's still not texting me back."

"Nope, nothing yet, but I'm sure she's just somewhere cooling off. I'll see you in a minute."

Chapter Thirty-Five
Monica

S itting outside the house of one of the first men Monica had ever loved...or at least thought she did, she went back and forth in her head about knocking on his front door. She had already gone through two bottles of wine before hopping in her car and making her way to his neighborhood. It wasn't in her plans to run to the man who almost destroyed her entire life, but after her fight with Nikki, she didn't know where to go other than back to the liquor store for some cheap wine that was going to leave her with a massive headache.

Monica was supposed to meet up with Rebecca to help her pick out an outfit for Nasir's baby shower, but if she was being honest with herself, she was pissed off with Rebecca for allowing Nikki to even discuss their business on a podcast. Even if people didn't know it was about her, Rebecca should've known that it would get to her. At this point, Monica wasn't happy with anyone, and they were the last people she wanted to be around.

What the fuck? Did you just forget about our plans? A text from Rebecca flashed across her screen, followed by another from Nikki apologizing for her feelings and expressing how

156

much she loved her. Monica wasn't sure what to say. She wanted to cuss both of those bitches out, but she knew not to do anything she would regret, which should have stopped her from stumbling her drunk ass to her ex's front door...but it didn't.

Standing at his doorstep, Monica flashed back to the day Darren called it quits. It was March 9, 2014. She was standing in the same spot when Darren made it clear as day, with his wife standing by his side, that he was no longer getting a divorce, and she had to get her things and go. He had bought a home for them to share, and despite finding out that he was married a year into their relationship, Monica still moved in with him.

During the time they were together, he gave her everything she wanted, and by the time they moved into the house, she was convinced divorce papers were sure to follow. They had been together for three-years, but it turned out that he was living a double life. The time he spent away from her was time he spent trying to win his wife back.

Monica always wondered what her life would've been like if Darren's wife didn't forgive him for stepping out on her.

"...why the fuck are you here?" a short petite woman asked, burning a hole through Monica with her eyes.

The sound of the woman's voice snapped Monica back into reality. It was Darren's wife, and she looked like she hadn't aged a day. She still had that same *I'm better than you'll ever be* look on her face that sent Monica into a jealous rage.

"This is *my* fucking house," Monica said, pushing past her. "Darren! Darren, where the fuck are you? Come down and face me like a real man," she yelled, as she ran up the stairs.

"Bitch, are you crazy?" his wife asked, as she grabbed Monica's arm, causing her to fall a few steps. "You need to get the fuck out of my house before I call the cops on you."

"Please, just tell me where he is," Monica cried, hysterically. "I need him to explain why he left me broken, unable to find the love he once gave me."

"He's not here, and you shouldn't be either. I don't know what you thought the two of you had, but he ended it five years ago when he sent you packing. It's over, Monica," she said, walking towards the door. "Now, get your crazy, drunk-ass off my floor and get out of my house, so I can go pick up my kids."

"Kids?" Monica asked, confused.

Darren always told her that he didn't want any children, and because she was so in love with him, she agreed that they would be fine without them.

"Yes, a four-year-old boy and a two-year-old girl," she responded with a grin on her face.

Feeling extremely embarrassed, Monica picked herself up off the floor and made her way back toward her car.

She was pregnant, she thought to herself, as she started her car.

Just as she was about to pull off, she saw an all-black Mazda CX9 pull into the driveway. Knowing she should've driven off, she watched as a tall white man with tattoos covering both of his arms, stepped out of the car and walked toward the woman. It was Darren, the one man she genuinely loved.

Besides his infidelities, he was nothing like the many men that followed. He was kind, attentive, and supportive, and he never laid a hand on her. It wasn't until his wife came back around that he switched up.

Watching the way he wrapped his arms around her as he brought her in for a hug made Monica realize she did have someone who made her feel like he used to, and she was all hers. She didn't have to worry about Nikki running back to an old love or living a double life. Nikki accepted Monica for all she was, and here she was about to ruin it all for a man who had built a relationship with her based on a lie.

The tears finally stopped rolling down her eyes, and the closure she thought she was going to get from Darren, she got right there in that car.

Taking one last look at what could've been hers, right then, she locked eyes with Darren and saw that sparkle that made her fall in love with him the first time around. She smiled at him, a smile that assured him that she had finally forgiven him.

"It's time for me to go get my woman back."

Chapter Thirty-Six

Ashley

"I'm so glad you're here; it's been forever."

"I know. I've been so caught up with work and my siblings. Shit is way more exhausting than I thought it would be," Brittney said, helping Ashley up off the ground.

"Thank you, girl," Ashley laughed, as they both struggled to lift her up. "I'm big as a house now...but trust me, I know what it's like having to look after your siblings. They become *your* kids, but it's better to be overwhelmed than wondering if they're getting their ass beat...or worse."

"You're right about that," Brittney said, walking over to the sofa to take a seat.

"How's Regina been doing? I haven't really bothered checking in on her because she's always on top of her shit."

Ashley knew she could trust Regina when it came to covering her workload. She was always on top of things—never missing an appointment or deadline. Plus, she was damn-near the only person in the office who their boss actually liked. There was no way she was going to drop the ball when it came to picking up extra caseloads.

"Uh...," Brittney said with a little hesitation. "For the most part, she's great, but today, she was supposed to come do one of those checks..."

"A welfare check?" Ashley interrupted.

"Yeah, one of those, but a few minutes before she was expected to show up, I got a call that she wasn't feeling well, and she needed to reschedule."

"...that's a first," Ashley mentioned, sounding a bit concerned.

Regina *never* missed a day of work, not even when she was sick. That woman would be at her desk with a shitload of cough drops, Theraflu, water, tea, and whatever else she thought would get her through her 8-hour day.

"Well, hopefully, she's okay."

"Um, she would want to be. She needs to be at my baby shower tomorrow."

"I know you're excited to have all your family and friends come to town and finally get all this planning over with." Brittney looked at all the decorations Ashley had lying around.

"You have no idea how ready I am for all this to be over with," she said, rubbing her stomach. "Maybe then Nasir will stop being such an asshole all the time."

Just as Ashley was about to start going in on Nasir and everything that had been frustrating her lately, the doorbell rang.

Speaking of the devil, she thought, as she went to open the door.

"Forgot your key again?" she shouted.

"Well, I see you weren't expecting me just yet," Nasir's mother said, with a smile on her face.

"Mrs. Wright." Ashley leaned in to give her a hug. "I was not expecting you just yet. I thought your son was going to pick you up and take you around town?"

"Well, you know that son of mine…"

She looked around the house in amazement. She knew her son had come along way, but she didn't know that he was living like this. As close as Nasir was to his mother, he rarely allowed her to come to L.A. For the most part, he always drove home to spend the holidays and special occasions with her, but the minute his business really picked up, those visits became less and less frequent.

Not like I used to, Ashley thought to herself, closing the door behind her.

"Can I get you something to drink?"

"Girl, if you don't sit your pregnant-ass down. I got this," Mrs. Wright said, rolling her bag into the living room. "And who might this pretty young lady be?" she asked, walking towards Brittney.

"Hi, I'm Brittney. Nice to meet you."

"Don't be shy, give me a hug…will you be staying for dinner? I just had that handsome driver my son sent to pick me up go on a grocery run. I'm going to make Nasir's favorite meal," she said, sitting down next to Brittney.

163

"A meal he doesn't deserve," Ashley mumbled under her breath.

"What was that, sweetie?"

"Oh, nothing, Mama," Ashley smiled.

"I would love to, but I actually need to go get these favors to the planner for Ashley and then get home to my brother and sister," Brittney said, grabbing her purse and the boxes of favors Ashley had stored away, hoping to make a quick exit before things got awkward. She could feel the tension in the air the minute Ashley saw Nasir's mom at the door.

"Well, will I see you at my grand baby's shower?"

"Of course!"

"You sure you can't stay a little longer?" Ashley looked at Brittney with desperation in her eyes. She was not ready to be left alone with Nasir's mother. It had been over ten-years since they had last seen each other.

Still annoyed with Nasir, she was in no mood to play catchup with his mother, yet alone watch her cater to him like he was a toddler.

"I would, but I still need to figure out what I'm wearing to this baby shower of yours. Plus, you should spend some quality time with your future mother-in-law," Brittney giggled, as she made her way towards the door.

"Hilarious."

164

Chapter Thirty-Seven
Nikki Shay & Rebecca

I know you're mad at me right now, but I'm worried about you. I'll be at Brandon and Rebecca's if you decide you want to talk.

Nikki sent Monica a text before getting out of the car. She couldn't believe they were going through a breakup over something they could have easily dealt with, with a bit of patience and understanding. Monica was the type to always get her way and rarely put herself out there. Nikki knew that, but from the many conversations she had with Rebecca, she figured things had changed.

"Wassup, Nik?" Brandon asked, opening the front door. He spotted her pull up on the camera he had installed. "It looks like you can use a drink."

"Now, you know I can *always* use a drink," she laughed, as she entered.

Heading downstairs to the movie theater, Nikki was starting to hope Rebecca was getting closer to the house before she and Brandon got too deep about what was going on in each other's lives. The only outcome of that conversation was Nasir coming up.

"So, what got you looking so sad?"

Brandon was behind the bar pouring a shot for himself and Nikki.

"What makes you think I'm sad?" Nikki smiled, awkwardly.

"You've been around long enough for me to notice when the smile on your face isn't genuine." He passed Nikki her shot.

"Observant...I see why Rebecca loves you," she said, hoping to change the subject.

"Yeah, I'm a pretty good guy."

"You better be, because she deserves nothing but the best."

"And the best is what she's getting," he said, finally taking his shot.

"Wasn't ready for that one, were you?" Nikki laughed at Brandon as he grabbed his chest and squinted his eyes from the fiery liquid.

"Anyway, you just trying to change the subject."

"Did it work?"

"*Nope,* but I'm not gon' press you...want one more shot before I head upstairs to mind my business? Babe should be here any second."

"Yes, please."

"...can I get one of those too?"

Rebecca came walking out of the elevator looking like a runway model. The way she stared at Brandon as she made her way to his side of the bar made Nikki miss Monica a tad bit more than the hour before.

"Anything for you," he said, pulling Rebecca in by the waist and shoving his tongue down her throat.

"Uh, should I give you two some alone time?" Nikki asked, as she watched Brandon and Rebecca make out like two teenagers.

"My bad. I just missed my girl...I'm about to get out of here."

"Don't go too far," Rebecca winked, planting one more kiss on Brandon before he made his way upstairs.

Before saying another word, Rebecca took her shot and then went on to make her and Nikki a Hennessy Margarita. She wanted to make sure Brandon was completely out of the room before they started having girl talk.

As much as she loved her some Brandon, she was still a little fucked up about that stupid-ass question Nasir left her with. Plus, she wanted to get into what happened between Nikki and Monica before she spat her thoughts about Nasir all over Nikki.

"So, what happened?"

"Oh, you waste no time, huh?" Nikki asked, adjusting herself in her seat.

"You know I don't, but I'm trying to figure out what the hell I did to her."

"She's upset about the podcast. Way more upset than I think she should be, but let her tell it, I disrespected her," Nikki said, shaking her head. "Let me start from the beginning..."

"Please do," Rebecca said, sipping on her drink.

"So, after we did the whole podcast and vlog thing, I took your advice and decided to go talk to Monica about our problem and give her a heads-up about the episode we recorded, so she wouldn't be caught off guard and catch another attitude. So here I go calling her phone back-to-back hoping to catch her before she left the house."

"Was she not staying with you last night?" Rebecca asked, confused.

The two of them practically lived together, even if Nikki didn't want to make it official, but Nikki had yet to tell her that Monica hadn't been back to her place since the night Monica first brought up the idea of them moving in together. Nikki thought Monica just needed her space, but she knew all too well what happened when too much space was given. Lesbians moved on quicker than the speed of light.

"I might have left out the part where she walked out on me the night before we recorded the podcast."

"*Nikkkkiiii...*"

"I know...I know. I thought it would blow over, but it didn't," Nikki responded, dropping her head.

Trying to stop herself from crying, she said, "I get to her place and grab the spare key that she keeps under the flowerpot next to the door. I walk in, and she's fully dressed, getting ready to go to the gym. She looks at me like, *wtf are you doing in my house?* and then proceeds to try to push me out the door. I couldn't let that happen before I said what I needed to say, so I stood my ground, which only pissed her off more, but she eventually sat down and listened to what I had to say. I went on to tell her about the show and my reasoning behind why I was scared for us to move-in together. But before I could even get out the words, 'I'm willing to take that chance,' she started to go off on me."

"Please, don't tell me it got physical." Rebecca got out of her chair to pour another drink.

Monica was good for throwing a fist when she felt disrespected. It didn't matter if it was a man or a woman, she stayed on go. Rebecca just prayed that wasn't the outcome though; this wasn't the time for her to be stuck between her best friend and her business partner, especially with their new book on the way.

"Oh, trust, it got really close. That woman was all up in my face, yelling about me comparing her to the next bitch, and how it was foul for me to have a conversation with you and all the world before coming to her about how I was feeling. The only thing that stopped me from putting my hands on her was the love I have for her, and I felt where she was coming from about not being an adult and coming to her. My ex did the same shit to me."

By time Nikki was done telling her story, she was crying like a baby on Rebecca's shoulder.

"What if I've lost her for good?"

"Think positive, Nikki. She'll come around. If I know anything about my best friend, I know for sure she loves you. If she didn't, she wouldn't be this upset."

"Are you sure? I don't want to go through losing another woman I love."

"I'm sure. Dry those eyes and have faith that everything will work out the way it's supposed to," Rebecca said, pulling Nikki in to comfort her.

"Kind of like you and Brandon," she said, leaning back.

"*Exactly* like that."

Chapter Thirty-Eight
Rebecca & Brandon

After consoling Nikki, Rebecca walked her to the car and finally made her way to the room to take a shower. Brandon had fallen asleep watching a documentary, waiting for her to come upstairs. He didn't expect Nikki to stay as long as she did, but he knew she needed to vent to someone from the sadness in her eyes—it was the same look Rebecca had when she was going through her breakup with Nasir.

Rebecca looked at Brandon and knew she had to tell him about her run-in with Nasir before they stepped into the baby shower. Her first thought was to keep it a secret, but after talking to Nikki, she knew she needed to be open and honest if she wanted her relationship to work. Brandon and Nikki were the only two people who had her back when Nasir dogged her out, and now, it was time to show her loyalty to Brandon. It was time for her to stop dwelling on what *could've* been when it was no longer...and for a good reason.

Before heading into the bathroom, she placed her phone on the charger, then walked over to Brandon to plant a kiss on his forehead.

I love you, she whispered in his ear.

"I love you more." He grabbed her and pulled her down onto the bed. "'Bout time you came to bed."

"Not just yet," she said, lifting herself. "I'm going to take a nice hot shower. I've been out all day."

"Want me to join you?" he asked, attempting to get out of bed, but Rebecca pushed him back down.

"Just relax. I need to get a little self-care in, and then I need to talk to you about something," she said, getting up, but Brandon grabbed her hand before she could completely walk away.

"Are we good?"

"We're better than good; we're great." She kissed him once more before heading to the bathroom.

Looking over at Rebecca's phone, which was lighting up in the corner, he thought about looking to see who was blowing her up.

Nah, B, it ain't even that serious, he thought to himself. *If she said we're good, we're good.*

Scrolling through Netflix, Brandon put on a random movie and waited for Rebecca to come out of the bathroom, which was taking forever. If she took any longer, he was going to be asleep again, and whatever she had to say was going to have to wait until the morning.

Rebecca stood in the shower, letting the warm water run over her hair and down her curvy body. She figured she'd wash her hair and wear it natural for the baby shower, but really, she was trying to avoid the conversation she needed to have with Brandon for as long as she could. The thought of telling him about Nasir still having feelings for her was a bit terrifying. The two of them had just made up with each other, and this was just another thing that could make everything go completely left...including her relationship. It wasn't like she wanted to be with Nasir, but she couldn't help but entertain the idea of *what if.*

Turning off the shower, Rebecca wrapped a towel around herself, dried off her hair, and walked to the mirror where she took one more look at her bare face.

"Bout time you brought yo' ass out of there...had me worried."

"I'm sorry, babe. I figured I'd get myself together for tomorrow."

"You ready for that? I know it might be a little awkward," Brandon said, sitting up.

"Honestly?" she asked, walking over to her dresser to slip on one of her sexy nightgowns.

"I wouldn't have asked if I didn't want to know."

"Okay, smart-ass...that's kind of what I needed to talk to you about," she said, approaching the bed. "I saw Nasir today."

Not knowing what was about to come out of Rebecca's mouth, Brandon braced himself for the worst. When it came to those two, anything was possible. Rebecca may have been with him now, but that couldn't take away the fact that Nasir had her first.

"So wassup? Is there something I need to know?"

"I know you and Nasir are getting your friendship back in order, but before we see him tomorrow, I need to let you know that...he still wants to be with me." She wanted to be straightforward. There was no point in sugarcoating the situation.

"Did he say those words out his mouth?"

"Not exactly like that, but he did ask me if I ever think about if we had stayed together."

"And?"

"And what?"

"Rebecca, don't act dumb."

"I'm not acting dumb," she said, walking towards him. "I told him that he needs to worry about his woman."

"Okay, but do you think about if you would've stayed with him?"

Brandon already knew what her answer was. Of course, she had thought about what it would be like to still be Nasir Wright's woman. After all, Brandon had a friendship with Rebecca before they became a thing, and he damn near knew everything about their relationship. If Nasir hadn't run into Ashley, he'd still be with Rebecca right now. Shit, if Ashley wasn't having his baby, he still might've had a chance with her. Brandon wasn't going to ignore the fact that he lucked up because his homie fucked up.

Chapter Thirty-Nine
Nikki & Monica

It wasn't in Nikki's plans to end up at Rebecca's crying over Monica all night, but it was exactly what she needed. Having someone she could lean on during tough times was something she was extremely grateful for. Nikki barely had any friends in L.A., let alone family, but Rebecca was the closest it came to having a best friend and sister. There was Monica, but right now, she didn't know where they stood.

All day, Nikki had been looking at her phone hoping to hear from Monica, yet her phone was still dry as ever.

Maybe, she is over me, she thought, as she pulled into her parking space, dreading the headache she was going to have from all the crying and shots she had taken earlier.

Before getting out of the car, she pulled out her phone to let Rebecca know that she had made it home in one piece and to thank her for listening to her. Nikki just hoped that she hadn't ruined any plans Brandon may have had for them.

Walking into the building towards her front door, she was sad about having to go to sleep alone...again—something she hadn't done in months.

176

Getting closer to her apartment, she noticed a body sitting directly in front of her
door, which appeared to be lifeless. Feeling
anxious and afraid, Nikki pulled out her
phone and began to dial 9-1-1 until she got
closer and noticed it was Monica knocked
out, smelling like nothing but alcohol.

"Get up...*now!*" she screamed, no longer
concerned, but angry and embarrassed.

*How long has she been waiting out here? How
many people just walked right past her?*

"Come on," Nikki said, trying to lift
Monica off the floor. "Please..."

"I'm trying," she mumbled, as Nikki
managed to lean her up against the wall to
unlock the door. "I'm *sooooo* sorry," Monica
said, falling against her. "Please, take me
back."

"Hurry up and get in here before any
more of my neighbors see you looking like a
fucking fool."

Nikki wanted nothing more than the
woman she loved to show up at her doorstep, begging for her forgiveness, telling her
how wrong she was and that she loved her.
Nikki knew she wanted to work things out
with Monica, but this was not how she had
imagined it.

"...please, forgive me," Monica said,
grabbing her by the face, and trying to kiss
her.

"What is wrong with you? This is what
you've been doing all day? It took you getting drunk to try and have a conversation...?

177

I don't want to talk to you until you sober up," Nikki said, pulling Monica towards the bedroom. "You can sleep in here. I'll take the couch."

"Stay with me, please. I need you...not just tonight, but always."

Without responding, Nikki sat Monica down on the bed and walked over to her dresser to pull one of her t-shirts out of the drawer. After getting her dressed, Nikki washed her face and forced her to take some Advil before she laid her down. She knew in the morning Monica would have a horrible headache and wouldn't remember anything about the day she had.

Chapter Forty
Nasir & Ashley

"You just going to keep on disrespecting me?"

It was midnight, and Nasir was just getting home.

"Every time I think we're on our way to being on the right track, you do some stupid shit to piss me off. I wish I didn't even have to deal with you tomorrow," Ashley said, pushing him into the wall.

"Calm down before my mom hears you."

"Fuck *you* and your *fake-ass* mama," she yelled. "I'm tired of you, and I'm tired of her."

While Nasir was out "working," Ashley had to listen to his mom talk about what was expected of her as a woman. Ashley always thought Mrs. Wright liked her, but all she saw was a charity case, a little girl who needed to be saved. And, as a grown woman, she didn't think of her any different. To his mother, Ashley finally got everything she always wanted—a good family to be a part of, a successful man to impregnate her, and all the material things her abused mother could never provide.

"Wow," Nasir said, walking into his closet to undress.

"Yeah, I said it. Fuck y'all!" Ashley repeated.

"You lucky you're carrying my son," he said, turning around and walking past her.

"…or what?"

"You don't want to find out," he mumbled under his breath.

"I heard that, asshole."

"Would you like a cookie…? Like I said, calm down before you wake my mom and upset my son."

"Whatever, Nasir! I have a long day ahead of me tomorrow…or did you forget that we have a baby shower we have to host?"

Not wanting to argue anymore, Nasir walked into the bathroom and started the shower. He'd make up with Ashley the best he could in the morning, but tonight, all he wanted to do was relax and try to clear his mind.

Chapter Forty-One
Morning of the Baby Shower

Derek & Nicole

"Uh, uh," Nicole said, jumping out of the bed. "Don't be trying to sneak out of this house like you do every Saturday. We have plans, *remember?*"

"Babe, I remember. I just need to run something to my office, and I'll be right back."

"Derek, I'm sure it can wait. Please, just do what I need you to do...for once. You can get back to work after today."

Nicole knew if Derek walked out of that door, he wasn't going to return until Sunday evening, a routine she had gotten accustomed to. First, she was clueless, but she had to stop the denial and accept things for what they were—he wasn't as affectionate as he used to be, he was becoming more aggressive towards her, and he seemed like he never wanted to be around. The only answer to the change in him had to be another woman.

181

Let's Be Friends…Again

"Let's just make it through today like a normal couple and then…"

"Then, what?" Derek interrupted.

"And then you can go doing whatever it is that you like to do," she said, patting him on the shoulder.

"What's that supposed to mean?"

"Nothing.

*****

Regina & Gary

Regina woke up to another delicious meal from the man she loved. After what happened with Shantel the previous morning, Gary had been catering to her every need, doing his best to make sure she was in a better mood for the day.

"Thank you, babe, but you didn't need to," Regina said, kissing him.

"Woman, you have got to start accepting the good in your life. I know you aren't used to getting this sort of treatment, but get used to it," he said, pulling her in tight.

"It's a process, but I promise I'm getting there."

"You sure?"

"I'm positive," she smiled, kissing Gary once more before sitting down to eat.

"Good," he smiled.

"Speaking of being positive, how do you think Brandon and Nasir are going to get along today?"

"*Shiiitt,* I'm more interested in seeing how Ashley is going to react to seeing Rebecca again," he laughed. "The last time I saw those two next to each other, Rebecca was ready to hop over a table."

"Lord, please, don't let this be a baby shower from hell, because I've had enough drama."

*****

Kim & Nick

"You sure this is the best place for me to be meeting your sister for the first time?"

"If we don't do it today, then who knows when I'll get the chance to do it again. She's about to pop, and I know once that baby comes, she's not going to want to deal with anyone," Nick responded. "Plus, she's been begging to see me, so I couldn't say, 'no' when she sent the invite."

After getting locked up, Nick started to distance himself from his sisters and friends. The distance made him step up as a man, especially after meeting Kim. He knew if she was going to take him seriously, he had to get his shit together and stop depending on his sisters for everything. It wasn't a good look anymore, and he got tired of everything being thrown back in his face, especially from Nicole. Every chance she got, she found a way to belittle him and make him feel like he wasn't worth a damn. It was crazy because they used to be inseparable.

"Okay, and what about Nicole? I know she doesn't like me," Kim rolled her eyes.

"Man, fuck her. She doesn't like anybody but that cheating-ass nigga she's about to marry. Just ignore her ass."

"All right. I'm about to get up so I can feed Ari and get her ready for my mom's."

"Let me slide up in that first," Nick said, pulling Kim back down onto the bed. "It's not like she's up yet."

"Be quick."

"Now, you know ain't nothing quick about me," he smirked.

Chapter Forty-Two
Brandon & Rebecca

REbecca wasn't looking forward to attending the baby shower. Brandon had seen right through her when she told him that she didn't care about Nasir. He tossed and turned for most of the night until grabbing a throw blanket to sleep in another room. Part of her wanted to run after him and start an argument, but the other half wished she hadn't said a word about Nasir. If they were going to make their relationship work, Rebecca knew she had to be honest. It was better for him to hear from the woman he sleeps with every night than the man she used to love. Secrets had ruined all her past relationships, and she wouldn't allow them to ruin another one.

As tired as Rebecca was from lack of sleep, she still managed to wake up at 5 a.m. and take her morning run. It was quieter than usual for a Saturday morning, but Brandon lived in a calm neighborhood.

Rebecca let the cool air brush across her face and travel through her hair. The beads of sweat dripping down her body felt like ice being rubbed across her skin. The faster she ran, the freer she felt. She didn't want to turn back, but she had to go home and face her problems head-on.

Walking into the house, she expected to see Brandon sitting on the couch with a fresh-made smoothie in hand with his music playing, but instead, it was extremely silent. The feeling of an empty house didn't sit right with her. Rebecca wanted to discuss last night's conversation, but today wasn't the day. Instead, she made her way to the kitchen and began to cook breakfast.

This should count for something.

Rebecca plated his French toast, bacon, eggs, and potatoes as fancy as she could and placed the plate on the dining room table with a cute note.

"A meal fit for a king," she said to herself, grabbing a piece of bacon.

Right as Rebecca was making her way to the bedroom, she could hear Brandon coming up the elevator, but she rushed upstairs to avoid speaking.

Brandon could hear Rebecca scurrying away, and it made him laugh a little. As mad as he was, he couldn't see a future without her.

Connecting his phone to his Bluetooth, he put on his favorite playlist. The first song to come blaring out of the house speakers was "Lady" by D'Angelo. He knew once his music started playing that it was going to be a good day.

Looking at the table, he saw the breakfast Rebecca cooked for him—still hot.

Sitting down, Brandon took a sip of his coffee, and that's when he finally saw the note.

The Universe knew what she was doing when she connected the two of us. If I could go back, I wouldn't change a thing, because I would have never met you. There is no doubt in my mind when it comes to the way I feel about you. I love you, and I will always choose you. Even in my darkest times, I know to look towards you to find the light.

Your Honeybee

Stuffing some bacon and French toast into his mouth, Brandon put the letter down and ran upstairs, where he found Rebecca in the bathroom taking a shower.

"What the hell, B?" Rebecca screamed, as he pulled the shower door open.

"I'm sorry," he said, stepping inside.

"Can't we talk about this *after* I get out? You know...when I'm not naked?"

"No," he said, grabbing her face. "I should have never second-guessed the way you feel about me. I love you, and I never want to give up what we have."

"I love you too, Brandon."

Getting down on his knee, Brandon pulled the engagement ring he had bought Rebecca out of the pocket of his basketball shorts. This wasn't how he planned on proposing to her, but at that moment, he couldn't wait any longer. Brandon knew he wanted to spend his life with her, and if what she wrote to him was true, that's what she wanted too.

"Brandon, what are you doing?"

"What I should have done a long time ago…Rebecca Bloom, will you do me the honor of being my wife?"

Rebecca, shocked by everything that was going on, stood there in silence as water poured down her body.

"…is that a 'no'?" Brandon asked, nervously, as water splashed on his face.

"*Yes!* I mean 'yes,' I'll marry you," she said, putting out her hand, so he could place the ring on her finger.

"You just made me the *happiest* man in the world," Brandon said, grabbing her by the waist and pulling her closer.

Lifting her leg onto his shoulder, Brandon began kissing Rebecca's inner thigh, making his way to her glistening lips. Her head tilted back, and she let all the tension in her body go as Brandon licked her clit and massaged her breasts with his free hand. She was completely his and was going to let him please her in every way he wanted to for the rest of their lives.

Chapter Forty-Three
Ashley & Nasir

"Change of plans. You can meet me at the venue around 11 a.m."

Ashley planned on arriving at her baby shower fashionably late, but after her fight with Nasir and him lying about where he was, she wanted nothing more than to get out of the house as soon as she could.

"I can be there. Is everything okay with the decorators?" Brittney didn't plan to go check on the setup until an hour before the shower started. Ashley wanted her to make sure everything looked fine before the guest arrived.

"Yeah, I'll fill you in later, but I need to get out of this house ASAP."

"Okay, I'll see you at 11 a.m., and I'll have a strawberry milkshake waiting for you."

"I knew there was a reason I loved you so much," Ashley smiled before hanging up.

Once she got off the phone, Ashley sent out a few texts to her hairstylist and makeup artist to see if they could also come to the venue instead. When she got confirmation from both, she took a quick shower, threw

189

on a tank and sweats, then packed up her baby shower outfit.

"Where are you going?" Nasir asked, walking into the room.

"To the venue to get ready."

"...but I thought we were going together?"

"I have a few things to look over, so everyone is meeting me there around 11 a.m. I already called a driver...just make sure you and your mom arrive on time." Ashley grabbed her bag before kissing Nasir on the forehead, leaving him confused. He wasn't sure if she was upset...or plotting ways to kill him later.

"Uh...okay. Let me know when you make it safe."

"I sure will."

I can't stand him, she thought to herself.

Heading into the kitchen, Ashley grabbed one of the cookies she made off the counter and headed for the door but was stopped by Mrs. Wright.

"Are you in a better mood this morning?" she asked, standing there with her hand on her hip.

"Oh, much," Ashley responded.

"So, I should be expecting an apology then, right?"

"An apology for what?"

"I heard you and Nasir arguing last night."

"Oh," Ashley said, embarrassed. She knew she was wrong for disrespecting her, but she was fed up. If it wasn't one thing with that family, it was another.

"I do apologize, Mrs. Wright. I should've never spoken that way about you. Right now, Nasir and I are having some differences, and I took my feelings out on everyone. I hope you can forgive me," Ashley said, putting her head down.

"Despite what you may think," Mrs. Wright said, walking towards her, "I really do like you. You're beautiful, intelligent, speak your mind, and you're one of the strongest women I know."

"Thank you."

"Seriously, Ashley, I know you've been through a lot throughout your life. You and my son may not be in an ideal situation right now, but remember, we have always been there for you. It's up to you now if you want us to continue to be there...or if this is something you want to walk away from. No matter your choice, we will always be family," she said, rubbing Ashley's stomach.

"I hear you...but I have to get going. We can talk more about this later, but, today, let's just enjoy ourselves." Ashley hugged Mrs. Wright and then made her way to the awaiting car.

*****

Nasir

Nasir woke up with a bad feeling. Maybe, it was the argument he had with

Ashley or the embarrassing encounter he had with his ex.

Today, he just wanted to make Ashley as happy as he could, but he was starting to feel like that ship was sailing…and *fast*. Usually, she would fuss about him not being involved more in the planning for their baby and furthering their relationship, but this morning when she woke up, she acted like nothing was wrong—at all.

"Ma," Nasir yelled, making his way into the kitchen where she was cleaning. "Did Ash seem a little off to you?"

"You know damn well that woman is mad," she said, rolling her eyes. "She's about to pop, and your stupid-ass decided to come home past midnight and think she wasn't going to be upset. Now, you got me mad," she said, throwing a dish towel down on the counter.

"What are you mad at me for? I didn't even do anything," Nasir lied. He knew Ashley wasn't feeling secure, and up until yesterday, he wasn't sure she should be. Part of him thought that he still might've had a chance with Rebecca, but she made it clear that it was over.

"Son, come have a seat."

Grabbing her coffee, Mrs. Wright walked over to the couch where Nasir had made himself comfortable. For the most part, she had always stayed out of her son's love life. She was just happy she raised a successful black man, who she thought was more respectful and mature than he was behaving.

"Now, you know I'm not for the drama, and I didn't come out to L.A. for all this. I came to celebrate my grandbaby and what I *thought* was a happy couple," she said, getting straight to the point. "Why did you put this girl up in this big ole house if you weren't ready to settle down?"

"I am ready, Mom."

"Don't look like it, and it 'sho don't sound like it."

"I'm trying."

"Not hard enough. Have you ever witnessed your father coming into the house at all hours of the night...? No, you haven't."

"I know."

"And have you ever seen him give me a reason to think I wasn't the woman he wanted to spend the rest of his days with?"

"No, Mom. Dad cherishes the ground you walk on, even when you are on his last nerves," he laughed.

"So, you should know to do the same, especially if this is the woman you want to walk down the aisle with."

"I've been doing the best I can, Ma. I even rented out a whole restaurant for her. That shit...I mean, the *mess* was not cheap," he said, trying to make excuses.

"Well, then why is she so *tired* of yo' ass? It's not for no reason. I've been knowing that girl since she was a teenager, and it's clear she loves you."

193

"I love her too…"

"But?" his mother interrupted.

"But…I love Rebecca too," Nasir said, putting his head down.

"So, why are you wasting this poor girl's time? You know better."

"Because I know we can be good together."

"Well, if that's what you know, you need to push that other girl out of your mind and heart. Focus on the woman in *this* household, the one carrying your legacy. You two have a tough and long road ahead of you if you plan on making this relationship work."

"Yeah, I know," Nasir said, kissing his mom on the cheek.

"Plus, that other girl doesn't even want you. She looks better with Brandon anyway," she laughed.

"*Wow,* that's cold," he said, shaking his head. "How do you even know about them?"

"I'm not that old. I know what social media is."

"Well, you can tell them when you see them today."

"Today?" his mother asked, surprised.

"Yup, Ashley invited them to the baby shower."

"Oh, well, you better be on your *best* behavior," she said, getting up.

Chapter Forty-Four
Ashley & Brittney

Walking into the venue, Ashley was greeted by her decorator at the door.

"Let me grab those for you. You shouldn't have to lift a finger," she smiled while taking Ashley's bag and walking them to one of the spare rooms.

"Thank you. I can't wait to see what you guys created for today."

"Sadly, you'll have to wait until your guests arrive, so don't be trying to sneak a peek."

"Aww, just a little, like a quick glance," Ashley smiled.

"Trust me, it'll be worth the wait."

"I hope so," she smiled. "Oh, and if you see Brittney, the young woman who brought over some of the decorations, can you send her in here please?"

"Will do!"

Ashley hung her gown on the door to make sure all the wrinkles came out and then walked over to the sofa to rest her feet, which were swollen.

I knew I should've put on those slides instead of these Jordans, she thought to herself. *I hope my feet go down soon.*

195

Ashley had a few hours to spare before anyone arrived, so she decided to have a peaceful moment to herself. She put on some meditation music, laid back on the couch, and closed her eyes. Baby Nasir must've felt the calmness come over his soon-to-be mommy because, for the first time, he wasn't having a party in her stomach. For a second, his not moving frightened Ashley. She was so accustomed to him being active, but when she tapped on her stomach and he tapped back, she was at ease.

I wish my life was always this peaceful, she thought, while rubbing her stomach.

Just as she began to drift off into a deep sleep, Brittney came barging into the room, milkshake in hand and a big smile on her face.

"Wakey, wakey, Sleeping Beauty."

"*Ugh,* just a few more minutes," Ashley sighed.

"Fine, just because it's *your* day."

Brittney walked over to the couch and lifted Ashley's legs, so she could have a seat.

"You okay?" she asked, taking her feet to massage.

"I could be better," Ashley responded with her eyes still closed.

"So, how can we make that happen?"

Brittney was extremely grateful to have someone like Ashley in her life; she put others before herself and always had the best intentions. Brittney was able to take care of not only herself but her siblings because of

Ashley. It was time for somebody to take care of her. Ashley needed to be nourished from the roots up.

"I'll be happy when the baby comes, but honestly...having my independence back would make me even happier. I need to get back into the office and back to my other babies," Ashley said, sitting up.

"What else?"

"I want to drive myself around again in my car, and dating...I miss dating."

"You and Nasir don't go out anymore?" Brittney asked, surprised.

"Rarely. I feel like all we've been doing since getting back together is arguing. Then, he wants to turn me into some housewife, but that's just not me. I love our home. I love that we're having a child together, but I miss my independence, and I miss feeling wanted," Ashley continued.

"Coming from someone who knows how pure your heart is, you deserve everything you want, so if you can't get it from Nasir, best believe there is someone else who will give it to you," Brittney said, hugging Ashley.

"Excuse me...? Can we come in and get you dolled up for the day?"

Ashley's makeup artist and hairstylist were standing at the door.

"Hey!" she said, enthusiastically. "You can set up right over there."

"I'm going to go make sure the crew isn't fucking up anything while you get done up,"

Brittney said, getting off the couch. "And drink up before that shake gets all watered down."

"Thank you, Brit. I love you more than you know."

"I love you too, sis."

Chapter Forty-Five
The Shower

Two o'clock finally arrived, and guests were pouring in—on time, to Ashley's surprise. Even Nasir managed to show up on time, keeping guests and his mother occupied while Ashley's stylist made a few final touches to her hair and makeup.

The setup for the shower was better than Ashley could've imagined. Upon entry, guests were greeted with a wreath of mostly white balloons, a pinch of gold, and transparent letter boxes that spelled out *BABY*. Walking in, the middle of the room had round tables covered in beautiful white satin cloths and gold and royal blue crown centerpieces. To the left, towards the back, sat a backdrop covered in white rose petals and the words *Welcoming Baby Nasir* written in gold script. On each side of the background sat a white throne with gold trim, fit for the queen and king. In the middle of the chairs was a translucent glass table with golden legs set up for guests to place their gifts. On the other end of the room, the food table was made up with all of Ashley and Nasir's favorite treats.

"It looks like heaven in here. I love it!" Mrs. Wright said, looking up at the ceiling, which was covered with white balloons. "Now, did Ashley plan this baby shower, or you?" she laughed, hugging her son.

"It was all Ashley, but I see she planned this with me in mind."

"She knows you *very* well."

"That she does…you want me to make you a plate or anything before you have a seat?"

"No, I'm good, son. I'm going to go say, 'hi' to Gary and that beautiful woman he just walked in with."

"Please, don't scare her off. I think this is the first woman he's ever loved," Nasir smiled, as he waved to them before making his way around to thank the guests and the crew for coming out on their special day. The only people he dreaded seeing were Brandon and Rebecca, especially after Brandon texted him and told him to stay away from her.

Just as Nasir was about to grab himself a drink, Ashley came walking into the room looking like a goddess. She had a baby blue, V-neck, sleeveless, floor-length dress with a train and a crown made of flowers. The dress was simple yet fit for a bride. Everyone in the room had disappeared, and all Nasir could see was her.

"She's beautiful, isn't she?" Nicole said, snapping him out of his daze.

"Beautiful doesn't even do her justice." He reached in to hug her. "Glad you were able to make it," Nasir said to Derek, who was standing behind Nicole.

"You know how these women are. There wasn't a chance she was going to let me miss today."

"I'm going to go say, 'hi' to my sister," she said, rolling her eyes at Derek.

"Let's get you a drink." Nasir put his hand on Derek's shoulder.

"I'm going to need one to make it through this day," he said, looking back at Nicole.

"Hey, everyone," Ashley beamed, walking towards her throne. "Ready to have some fun?"

"You know we are," a few of the guests yelled out.

"Everyone, go ahead and get some food, and we'll get started in about twenty minutes," Brittney announced over the mic.

"You look amazing," Regina said, making her way over.

"Thank you, Gina...so do you." Ashley got up to hug her. "I'm so glad you made it on time."

"Oh, you got jokes. We all know you're the only one who stays on black people time."

"You ain't never lied," Nicole chimed in.

"Nice to see you again," Regina said, hugging Nicole.

"You too."

"I see you were finally able to get your fiancé out of the house," Ashley said, sarcastically.

"You can just pretend like he isn't even here...that's what I'm doing."

"Well, excuse me then," Ashley laughed. "Seems like we're all having a little drama with the men in our lives."

"At least your sister isn't trying to sleep with yours," Regina said, as she looked in Gary's direction.

"I know you lying," Ashley said, shocked. She knew Shantel was a mess, but she never thought she'd try to fuck over her sister.

"Yeah, I'll tell you *that* story another day."

After the girls chatted for a bit and the guests ate, Brittney went around to the tables to hand everyone a piece of paper, pencil, and envelope. She directed them to write a positive message that baby Nas could look back on when he got older. Ashley thought this would be a perfect way to remind him just how loved he was, something she wished was instilled in her as a young lady.

Once everyone's notes were finished, Brittney went around and collected them.

"All right, let the games begin," she yelled over the mic. "Which one of you men think you can change a diaper in under a minute?"

"Oh, I got this," Nick shouted from across the room.

"Come on up, baby brother," Ashley blurted out in excitement.

"You gonna be okay, baby?" Nick looked over at Kim and asked.

"Yeah, go on up. I'm going to grab a drink and try to find a seat."

Just as Nick kissed her and walked away, Kim felt a tap on her shoulder and a familiar voice.

"Hey, Kim," Brandon said, surprised to see her.

"Oh, my goodness," she said, hugging him. "What are you doing here?"

"You do know whose baby shower this is, right?"

"It's my boyfriend's sister. We haven't officially met yet...excuse my manners by the way. I'm an old college friend of Brandon's. My name is Kim," she said, reaching her hand out to give Rebecca a handshake.

"Nice to meet you, Kim. I'm Rebecca, Brandon's fiancée," she smiled, happy to have the title.

"You're *gorgeous.*" Kim examined her from head to toe. "You did an excellent job, Brandon."

"Ya' boy lucked up," he said, kissing Rebecca on the forehead. "Have you seen Nas and Gary yet?"

"Na-Na-Nasir?" Kim started to stutter.

"Yeah, this is his baby shower," Brandon informed her.

Looking over to her left, she saw Nasir center stage laughing it up with Nick. Kim wanted to run out of the door and make her way home, but she couldn't leave Nick. It was important to him that she finally meet his sister.

"Would you like to go get a drink?" Rebecca could see the fear in her eyes as she looked at Nasir.

"...she may need a few," Brandon whispered in her ear.

*****

Scared to find a table or take part in any of the activities, Kim remained by the open bar talking to Rebecca, who happened to be a breath of fresh air. She could see why Brandon put a ring on her finger.

In college, he was always into those pretty girls who kept their heads in the books, and he was quite intelligent himself from what she could remember. He was never in any trouble, instead, he was the one keeping those around him out of it. For a long time, Kim wanted to hold a grudge against him for simply being best friends with Nasir, but if it weren't for his help, she would've been stuck in a cycle of violence. The last thing he said to her before she disappeared was, "You deserve a love free of pain," and he was right.

As Kim and Rebecca sat there talking and sipping on wine, Kim started to realize that she had seen Rebecca before.

"...you look so familiar. Do you work at Pretty & Bold Publications?"

"Yeah. Now that you bring it up, aren't you Laura's sister?"

"That's me!"

"Sorry, we didn't get to formally meet yesterday. I was rushing out to find an outfit for this dreadful baby shower."

"Well, I think you look absolutely beautiful," Kim smiled. "And what's so dreadful about it?"

"Well, don't judge me when you hear this...but the baby daddy is my ex, and Ashley is the woman he cheated on me with. I'm only here because he and Brandon are trying to mend their friendship."

"I'm the last person to judge anyone. Funny story, the baby daddy is also my ex-boyfriend, and I had no idea this was his baby shower. Nick never brought him up."

"We may need something a little stronger to make it through this day."

While Rebecca was getting acquainted with Kim, Brandon went to announce his arrival to his brother.

"Bruh, you won't believe who is here right now."

"Who?" Regina jumped in, being nosy.

"Don't you have a game to play?" Brandon responded, hoping she'd get out of their business.

"You're rude...where is Rebecca, so I can talk to her?"

"By the bar."

205

"Man, why you gotta be rude to my girl like that?" Gary asked once Regina was out of earshot.

"Because I don't need her going back to Ashley telling her that *another* one of Nas' ex-girls is in the building," Brandon said, tilting his head in Rebecca's direction.

"…is that Kim?"

"In the flesh. I'm not in the mood to even be around Nasir, but I need him to stop playing *guess what's in the diaper*, so I can tell him wassup," Brandon continued.

"I can get him, but y'all still haven't told me what the big deal is," Gary snapped.

"The problem is he almost beat the life out of her in college. I'm surprised she hasn't run out of here yet."

"Damn."

"What you boys over here talking about?" Mrs. Wright came walking up to the table.

"Oh, nothing. We're just laughing at the fact that Nasir is the first to have a kid. I was sure it was going to be Gary," Brandon quickly said, changing the conversation.

"Well, I have an idea who's up next," she responded. "Where is that pretty ole Rebecca at?"

"You not going to cuss her out, are you?"

"Now, Brandon, who do you boys think I am? Nasir said the same thing when I went to introduce myself to Regina."

"My bad," Brandon laughed. "Rebecca will be happy to know you aren't upset with her.

"Like I told my son, I think you two are beautiful together, and he should have done right when he had her."

"Dang, you told him that?" Gary asked.

"Hey, I'm a woman, and I'm always going to tell that boy like it is."

"That's why we love you," Brandon added.

As she walked away, Brandon and Gary both walked over to Nasir to pull him to the side. He seemed to be having a good time celebrating with Ashley, and they wanted to keep it that way.

"You mind if we take him away for a minute?" Gary asked Ashley.

"Please do," she insisted. "He seems to be having more fun than I am. It's my turn...also, can you grab me an enchilada after you guys have your little chat?"

"I got you," Nasir said, kissing Ashley and rubbing her stomach before following Brandon and Gary toward the back.

"Before we make it to the food table, I need to give you a heads up...Kim is here," Brandon said, as calmly as he could.

"Are y'all trying to ruin my day?" Nasir asked, defensively. "What in the hell is she doing here?"

"From what I know, she's dating Nick. So, I suggest you figure out how to apologize as quickly and genuinely as you can, because she's going to be meeting Ash, soon," Brandon responded.

As they got closer to the food table, Nasir could see his mother and a few other women gathered around Rebecca smiling, laughing, and sharing hugs.

What are they all so excited about? he wondered.

But that thought didn't last for too long, because shortly after, he saw Nick coming his way with Kim on his arm.

"We'll leave you guys to talk," Gary said, as they approached Nasir. "That's all we needed to tell you."

"Good looking out."

"Wassup?" Nick said. "Aye, Nasir, I want you to meet my girl, Kim. I'm about to introduce her to Ashley before we get going. I think we've been here a little too long."

Thank goodness, Nasir thought to himself.

"I'm about to grab Ash some food...nice to meet you, Kim."

"So, are we going to play that game?" she snapped.

"What are you talking about, baby?" Nick asked, confused.

"This is the guy who put this scar under my eye," she said, pointing to her face.

Before Nasir could respond, Nick knocked him to the ground with one punch.

"Let's go," he said, grabbing Kim's hand.

"I'm sorry!" Nasir blurted out, trying to get off the ground.

"I should beat yo' ass. You no better than any of them men my mom had running in and out of our lives," Nick spat.

"Let's just go," Kim said, pulling Nick away. "He's not worth it."

Chapter Forty-Six
Ashley

The day started rough, but her baby shower was everything Ashley dreamed of. Everyone was having a good time playing the games Brittney set up, her brother and sister were getting along like the old days, but most importantly, Nasir was happy. Ashley felt part of a family, and she wanted that feeling to last forever.

When Rebecca arrived, Ashley spotted her walking towards the back, but she knew she had nothing to worry about. The way she was staring at Brandon was the exact look she gave Nasir, that *I'm in love and will never leave your side* look. Ashley figured she'd finally have that woman-to-woman talk with her. Maybe, that would be the answer to all her problems.

When Nasir walked away, there was one more game to play, guessing the size of Ashley's stomach. In the middle of being wrapped with ribbon, Ashley heard a bunch of commotion, and the crowd was starting to move towards the back. Hearing her brother's voice caused her to push through the group surrounding her as fast as she could.

"What is going on?" she asked, approaching her brother, who was ready to put Nasir back on his ass.

"Ask your baby daddy! I wanted to introduce you to the woman I love, but we can't stay here."

"Please, Nick, I need you here...can't we talk about this?" she asked, grabbing onto him.

"Sis, I promise we will talk about this later, but before I ruin your day any further, I need to get away from this woman beater," he said, looking over at Nasir.

"Woman beater?"

"Talk to *him*, sis," he said, giving her a long hug and a kiss on the cheek.

"...I hope to meet you once everything has calmed down," Kim added.

"What did you do?!" Ashley asked with tears rolling down her face.

"That was the old me."

"Did you hurt that woman, Nasir?"

"It was a *long*, long, time ago," he pleaded, walking closer to Ashley.

"You make me sick! You're such a fucking hypocrite. Nothing ever goes right with you around," she yelled before storming off.

Nasir attempted to run after her, but his mother stopped him in his tracks. As a woman, she knew everything that Ashley had to endure growing up, and the last person she was going to want to hear from was the man who did the same thing to someone else.

211

"There's nothing to see here," Gary and Brandon said, clearing everyone from around Nasir.

"Exactly! Move your asses," Mrs. Wright added. "There's plenty of food and drinks for you to enjoy."

The crowd scattered throughout the room, taking pictures at the photo booth, making plates, and dancing to the music the DJ started to play again. Nicole went to grab Derek and insisted that he help her start packing up all the gifts. There was no way in hell Ashley was going to be in any mood to open presents…especially not with Nasir.

"And you thought we had drama," Derek joked.

"This isn't funny. And, if we're being honest…we do."

"Which is what, Nicole?"

"I'll be staying with my sister in her guest room until you decide if you want to marry me…or be with that bitch you've been cheating on me with," she said, giving him her ring back.

*****

While Brittney kept the party going, Ashley was outside pacing back and forth, trying to compose herself, but she couldn't stop crying. She never wanted to imagine Nasir as *that* man, but now that she knew what he was capable of, how could she stay?

This is the sign I needed, she thought, as she sat down on a bench next to the building. *It's time for me to let this relationship go.*

"Do you mind if I sit here?"

Looking up, there was Rebecca. Ashley prayed she wasn't coming to gloat; it was the last thing she needed.

"...sure," she said, wiping away her tears.

Rebecca was standing front and center when everything happened and noticed how no one went running after Ashley. Everyone might have known it was better to keep the baby shower going and to let her gather herself first, but Rebecca knew that if it was her in that situation, she would want someone by her side.

"I know we've had our issues, but I wanted to make sure you and the baby were okay. That was a lot."

"Why do you even care? Don't you hate me?"

"Hate you? Never. Maybe, *dislike,* and these days, that's even a stretch," Rebecca admitted. "What happened with Nasir, I had nothing to do with you, but more so with him. I no longer have anything to be upset about," she said, placing her hand on top of Ashley's. "I forgive you."

"Really? When this baby drops, you're not gonna hop any tables if you see me out, are you?" she asked, jokingly.

"You have nothing to worry about," Rebecca said, squeezing her hand. "Now, are you sure you and the baby are good?"

"He's fine. I can feel him moving around in there. Me? My heart is breaking, but I'll be fine. I always am."

"Would you like to go back in and enjoy the rest of your day? I hear some music."

"Come on, let's go." Ashley stood up slowly and grabbed Rebecca's hand. "Let's show them how to have a good time…by the way, that's a pretty engagement ring."

The two of them walked back into the venue, and all eyes were on them, especially Nasir's.

For the rest of the baby shower, he didn't say a word; instead, he watched Ashley and Rebecca dancing around like they were the best of friends until he finally had enough.

Grabbing his keys and whispering "goodbye" to his mother, he quietly made his exit.

Chapter Forty-Seven
Brandon & Rebecca

Despite all the drama, everyone danced until it was time to walk out the door. The night was still young, so the twins and their ladies decided to hit the town for some food and drinks, just like old times. Rebecca wanted to celebrate her being the future Mrs. Young.

They decided to an intimate place, out of the way of all the action, including anywhere that Shantel may've gone to.

Rebecca still hadn't heard from Monica, but she wanted nothing more than to clear the air with her and get back to the way things used to be.

"I think I'm going to send a text to Nikki and Monica, so they can join us."

"Are they even on good terms right now? I know Nikki was going through it last night," Brandon said, making sure to keep his eyes on the road.

"That's why I'm going to send a group text…what's the worst that can happen?" she shrugged, as she pulled out her phone.

"They cuss you out, then cuss each other out," he laughed.

"Whatever. I'm in a good mood."

215

"I see that. Watching you and Ashley getting along like that was the last thing I expected to happen," Brandon looked over at her and smiled.

"I felt like she could use a friend. Besides, if you and Nasir are going to be friends again, it's for the best."

The car filled with silence, besides the sounds of smooth R&B playing. Brandon made a playlist just for Rebecca, so they wouldn't have to argue over his taste in music.

Brandon didn't want to admit that his friendship with Nasir was over, but he couldn't see them going back to the brotherhood they once had. Truth was, Nasir's life was falling apart, and no amount of money could make up for what he wanted—a life with the woman Brandon loved.

"Babe, that story is ending. I'm only looking forward to our future."

"It's bright," Rebecca said, lifting her hand to look at the mountain sitting on her ring finger.

Arriving at Firefly in Studio City, Brandon parked and waited for Rebecca to finish touching up her lipstick and curls before walking into the restaurant. Just as she opened the door, her phone went off. It was Nikki letting her know that she wouldn't be able to make it because Monica didn't feel good. The woman had drunk so much, Nikki was afraid she was going to have to take her to the hospital.

Although Rebecca was sad they couldn't make it out, she was happy to hear that they were together. She sent a text letting them know that she had something she wanted to share with them both; then she and Brandon went inside to meet Regina and Gary.

Walking inside, they headed to the outdoor dining area where Regina and Gary were sitting. Surrounded by trees and beautiful foliage, the area was lovely. Above them, you could see the sun as it set, and the room was dim, filled with hanging lights and candles at each table. Rebecca couldn't have thought of a better place to celebrate.

"Hey, *Mr.* and *Mrs.* Young," Regina yelled out, as they approached the table.

"Calm down, woman. They haven't walked down anybody's aisle yet. She might just drop his ass," Gary joked.

"With that rock on her finger? I doubt she's going anywhere."

"I see you have no faith in me as usual," Rebecca said, looking at Gary, as Brandon pulled out of her seat.

"Now, you know I'm playing. I'm happy for the both of you, happy to see my brother settling down."

"When you find that one, you gotta lock 'em down before it's too late," he said, glancing over at Regina.

"You're right about that one," Gary said, catching onto what his brother was implying, that he needed to be purposing next.

Waving the waiter over to the table, Brandon ordered two bottles of Pinot Grigio for a celebration toast and a tray of cheese and meats for the table. He also requested bread and butter to soak up the other cocktails the ladies ordered. Rebecca ordered a Wine on the Mind, which had white wine and rum in it, while Regina ordered a Pineapple Express that consisted of Grey Goose, pineapple juice, lemon, and elderflower liqueur.

"Oh, they about to show out tonight, mixing that wine and liquor," Gary grinned.

"Welp, my man deserves it all." Rebecca leaned over and forced her tongue down Brandon's throat.

"Okay, I'm not trying to see all that," Gary pretended to gag. "Save it for the honeymoon."

While waiting for their drinks and appetizers, Regina caught everyone up on the nonsense she and Gary had to deal with when it came to her sister. Although Brandon knew what happened, he pretended to be as clueless as Rebecca. Shantel had always been crazy and manipulative, but he never would've thought that she'd go that low. From the looks of things, Regina was done with her, but they still needed to run a business together.

In the middle of their conversations, Gary and Regina saw Nikki and Monica walking in. Brandon and Rebecca were in the opposite direction, so they couldn't see them coming in. Monica placed her finger to her lips before Gary could say anything.

Slowly creeping up behind Rebecca, she placed her hands over her eyes and yelled out, "Surprise!"

Shocked to see her best friend, Rebecca started to cry.

"I thought you didn't feel good?"

"I didn't, but there's no hangover in the world that would stop me from finding out what news my sis had for me," she smiled.

"The minute I told her you wanted to tell us something, she jumped up," Nikki added.

"Well, pull up a seat, because you're going to need one for this," Regina emphasized.

"Um, did we miss something?" Monica was ready for anything when it came to her best friend. "I know you guys all went to that baby shower today."

"Besides Ashley and Rebecca becoming friends and Nas getting punched out by his ex-girlfriend's new boyfriend, who also happens to be Ashley's little brother, you didn't miss a thing," Regina shook her head and laughed.

"That's a plot twist for real," Nikki chimed in.

"But that's *not* the news I wanted to share with you guys," Rebecca said, looking down at her hand.

Noticing two more guests at the table, the waiter grabbed two more glasses and headed over with a bottle of wine. He placed them down on the table and began to fill everyone's glass.

"I hope you enjoy it," he said before he walked away.

Picking up her glass, Rebecca grabbed Brandon's hand and began to speak.

"As you all know, Brandon and I have known each other for some time now, but it wasn't until last year that we realized we were meant for each other. And since making it official, we've had one hell of a ride."

"Tell me about it."

"You can say that again."

"Don't we know it?"

Everyone added their two cents before Rebecca could continue.

"Y'all funny," Brandon laughed. "Let my baby finish."

"Thank you, babe...like I was saying, we've had one hell of a ride, but it's not over because we're getting married!" Rebecca said, ecstatically, putting her hand out for Nikki and Monica to see.

Immediately, Monica began to cry, but they were tears of joy. Just like everyone else, she knew that Rebecca was finally going to get her happy ending, and she couldn't wait to help her plan the wedding.

"So, when are we getting started?" she asked.

"*ASAP!*" Brandon smiled, looking over at his wife-to-be.

Chapter Forty-Eight
Nasir & Ashley

Before walking out of the venue, Nasir looked back one more time at his glowing baby mother and blushing ex; it was time for a change.

There was no more hiding from his past; it was time to man up. Not only did he embarrass himself, but he also embarrassed his mother and made a fool of his woman on her special day.

Ashley had been through so much throughout her life, and he had a front-row seat to it all. To her, Nasir had always been an angel sent down from heaven, but the way she stared at him made him feel like the devil. He didn't know how he was going to face her when she arrived home. Part of him wanted to pack up his things and go stay at a hotel for the night, but he couldn't run away from his problems anymore. So, if that meant sleeping on the couch and dealing with Ashley ignoring him for the next few days, then that's what he was going to have to do.

"You good, boss?" his driver asked, looking through the rearview mirror.

"Yeah, I'm good," he said, looking out the window as they approached his home.

"I'm just ready to get all this stuff out of the car and into the house before I lay down."

When Nasir left the shower, he decided to leave his car with his mom and take the one Derek and Nicole had loaded the gifts in. The least he could do was get everything into the house and set up in their son's room for Ashley.

"So, how was that baby shower?"

"It was nice," Nasir responded, trying to avoid the conversation as much as possible. His eye was starting to swell, and he knew his driver was being nosy. If it wasn't for Ashley, he wouldn't've hired him, but he couldn't let her drive herself around pregnant.

"That's wonderful."

After getting everything unloaded, the driver went to park the car in the garage, then headed to his vehicle to leave, happy he didn't have to come back for a couple of days.

Walking past the gifts sitting in the doorway, Nasir looked around at his empty house and wondered if he would be okay living there alone. Looking around, he began to imagine Ashley sitting on the family room floor with a huge smile on her face, laughing and playing with their son as he watched from a distance. He knew Ashley was going to be a great mother, and he wanted to be there to experience every bit of it—the sleepless nights, the sore breasts, the days she's so tired she doesn't care about taking a shower, her being excited about his first words and steps, all the way up to her yelling from the stands on graduation day.

Coming out of the daydream he was in; Nasir went to the kitchen to grab an ice pack out of the freezer and then made himself comfortable in his favorite chair. As he laid his head back with the ice pack over his eye, his phone started to ring. Not wanting to speak to anyone, he didn't bother getting up to see who was calling.

Ring. Ring. Ring.

There was the sound of his phone again, and then he could hear a text.

On the fifth call, Nasir finally got out of the chair to answer his phone.

"Get your ass to the hospital now. The baby is coming!" his mom yelled.

"Oh, shit!" he said, rushing to the baby's room to grab the bag Ashley packed, and out the door, he went. "I'm about to be a dad."

*****

On their way out, Nick and Kim decided to go back to check on Ashley. Though Kim appreciated how he had stood up for her and wanted to make her feel protected, she felt horrible about ruining Ashley's day.

"You came back," Ashley shouted with joy.

"I didn't want to, but this woman right here convinced me to turn the car around."

"Are you okay?" Ashley asked Kim.

"I should be asking *you* that question. I had no intentions of coming here to start drama."

"This isn't your fault. Nasir should've been more honest about his past," Ashley said, grabbing her hand. "Can I ask you one question?"

"Anything."

"Was what he did to you a one-time incident?"

"Really, Ash? Do you need to know that to decide if you want to be with this fool or not?" Nick interrupted.

"She does," Mrs. Wright responded. "I'll be sitting by the entrance when you're ready to go."

Nasir's mom didn't want to hear anymore about her son's indiscretions.

"Like it or not, he's the father of your nephew, and as a family, we are going to have to get along...whether I'm with him or not," Ashley responded.

"It's okay, babe...yes, it only happened once, and I'm the only woman he has lost his cool with that I know of, but it traumatized me. He was a good guy until he started drinking, and he could be a great man today. What you do is all up to you," Kim said, grabbing Ashley's hand. She wanted her to feel how true her words were.

Hearing Kim's words made her feel like she hadn't completely lost Nasir to the dark side and that there was still some hope for her family. She still needed him to talk to

Nick about the situation to feel better, but they would have to save that for another day.

"I appreciate you being woman enough to come back here and talk to me. Also, it seems like you've gotten my hardheaded little brother to get his act together, and I'm so grateful for that," she smiled, as she wrapped Kim in her arms.

Just as she was about to let go, she felt a sharp pain shoot up her back. The pain almost brought her to her knees. All she could do was hold on to Kim for dear life as she felt another pain go up her back.

"She's in labor," Kim yelled, causing everyone to rush over to Ashley. "Sweetie, can you walk?"

"Yes, just get me to the car," she shouted.

"We're right here in the front," Nasir's mom said, pointing the key at the car to unlock the door.

"I'll drive," Nicole said, grabbing the keys.

"We'll meet you guys at the hospital," Nick added.

"I'm not ready. I still have a few more weeks." Ashley started crying through the contractions.

"You're going to be a great mother, Ash. Just breathe," Nick said, kissing her on the forehead before closing her door.

"Call Nasir...*now!*" she yelled, as they entered the freeway. "He's going to be a daddy."

Chapter Forty-Nine
Ashley & Nasir

The ride to the hospital was hell. Nicole bobbed and weaved through traffic as Mrs. Wright held onto the door for dear life. Ashley lay across the backseat, praying she didn't have her first child in a car; that was far from the birth plan she had in mind.

Ashley was hoping to go to her last appointment to see how she and the baby were coming along; they didn't even get the chance to pre-register at the hospital. The only part of her birth plan that was going right was her not using any medicine to help with her pain, but the way her contractions were coming, she wished she had something.

"Are we almost there?" she screamed, as another contraction came.

Her contractions were about three minutes apart, and the closer they got to the hospital, she was beginning to feel the urge to push.

"Just a few more minutes, baby. We're almost there," Mrs. Wright responded, calmly.

At that moment, Ashley wanted to call out for her mother, but she couldn't. This was the time in her life when she could've used her comfort, but she was blessed to have Nasir's mother by her side.

When they arrived at the hospital, Nasir was already waiting in front of a wheelchair and two nurses. Looking at him, there was no doubt in Ashley's mind that he was going to be an amazing father.

In the delivery room, Nasir was all she needed him to be, making sure her every need was met and assuring that she was as comfortable as she could be. He made sure her hair was tied up, the sweat was wiped off her face, and rode the wave of every contraction and hand-crushing squeeze.

When it was time for her to push, he talked her through it, held onto her leg for dear life, and once that beautiful head of hair began to show, he was the first to let his tears flow.

Giving birth to Nasir Jr. was the happiest moment the two of them had ever shared and Ashley wasn't sure if any other moment could top this.

Baby Nasir entered the world at 7 lbs. 8 oz., with his eyes wide open. He let out a strong cry but stopped as soon as he was placed into his mother's arms as if he was waiting to meet her.

"He's more than I dreamed of," Ashley said, admiring her creation.

"Thank you," Nasir whispered.

"For what?" she asked, without taking her eyes off her baby.

"For him," he said, looking down at their son. "And for dealing with all my bullshit. You deserve so much more than what I can give you."

"You've given me a lot, Nasir...I'm looking at him."

"But you deserve love, honesty, and commitment. You deserve to know the man I truly am, not the boy you fell in love with."

"We can always start over...as friends and see where it takes us."

"I'd like that," Nasir said, kissing her on the forehead.

"Should we let everyone in to meet the baby?"

"They can wait a little longer. I want to live this moment with just the three of us for a while."

*****

After spending two days in the hospital, Ashley and the baby were finally about to walk into their home. She was ready to take a nice long shower and relax in her king-sized bed before she found herself up all hours of the night taking care of the baby.

Before leaving the hospital, Ashley and Nasir agreed that a relationship wasn't what the two of them needed right now, but they would remain a family unit. Nasir offered to move to an apartment complex nearby, but Ashley felt like it would be better for him to stay in the house and just take one of the other rooms. Ashley wanted Nasir around their son as much as possible. They may not have been right for each other, but she knew they would make an unstoppable team when it came to parenting.

On top of them staying in the same house, they would also have help from Nicole, who decided to move in with them until she was able to get back on her feet. Ashley was shocked when she told her that she was leaving Derek and there wasn't going to be a wedding, but she was thrilled that her sister had finally come to her senses before she got stuck in a marriage neither of them wanted to be in. As for Derek, she prayed the woman he was running around with made his life a living hell.

"Happy to be home?" Nasir asked, opening the car door.

"You have no idea," she responded, as she reached over to grab the baby. "I am dreading getting his room together though."

"Don't worry about that right now. Let's just get you and the baby inside."

Grabbing Ashley's belongings, they both went headed inside. Nasir took out his keys and slowly unlocked the door. As soon as the door swung open, Ashley saw a *Welcome Home* banner, white and blue balloons everywhere, and a cake on the table she couldn't wait to stuff in her mouth.

"Surprise," everyone whispered in unison, which caused Ashley to break out into laughter.

"You guys, a little noise is not going to hurt the baby," she smiled and then continued to laugh.

"Oh, shut up and come show off that beautiful little boy," Nicole spat at her sister.

"Let me go get him changed, and I'll be right back."

"Don't take too long," Nicole replied.

"Keep that same energy when he needs a feeding or diaper changed in the middle of the night," Ashley murmured, as she walked away.

Walking into the nursery, tears filled Ashley's eyes. She saw a ton of new books and plush toys organized neatly on the bookshelf. Going through his drawers and closet, she noticed that everything had been washed and neatly put away. Everything she thought she needed to do was done—there was nothing left.

"You like it?" Nasir's mom asked, standing at the door and looking at Ashley. *Grateful* was written all over Ashley's face.

"Did you put all of this together?"

"I did, with the help of your sister. I hope you don't mind us opening the baby's gifts without you."

"With everything that's been going on, I'm more than okay with it. I was dreading having to do all of this and taking care of the little one. I would've never finished," Ashley said, pulling a newborn onesie out of the closet.

"Let me get him together for you," Mrs. Wright insisted.

"Are you sure?"

"I'm positive. Go get yourself showered and changed while I spend some time with my grandson before they all try to get their hands on him."

"Thank you...and thank you for being here. I wouldn't've been able to make it through this without your reassurance."

"I told you when you were a child, and I'm going to tell you again." Mrs. Wright reached out and grabbed Ashley's hands. "You can always call me for anything. We're family."

A tear fell from Ashley's eye, as she went in for a hug.

"I love you...Mom," she said, proudly.

"Am I missing something? Is there going to be a wedding?"

"I wish," Ashley laughed. "But Nasir and I decided that it's best if we start over as friends. And before you ask...no, he's not moving out."

"In the future?"

"Possibly, but we'll see," Ashley said, heading towards her room. "I'm going to take a shower now."

As she made her way down the hall, she stopped to peek into the living room.

"You good?" Nasir asked, sneaking up on her.

"I'm happy, truly happy."

"That's all I've ever wanted for you," he admitted, kissing her on the cheek, then walking back into the living room to chill with Gary.

Everyone she cared about was standing in the living room ready to celebrate her coming into motherhood. The differences between siblings and significant others were put to the side for the sake of the life she just gave birth to.

She watched as her sister sipped on her drink and joked with her brother like they did when they were kids. It had been months since she saw them both genuinely happy. Brittney and her siblings sat around the table with Regina playing Uno, while Nasir and Gary sat on the couch like two old men, drinking beer and watching TV. The sight was lovely, and Ashley wouldn't've had it any other way; she got everything she wanted…including her best friend back.

www.ingramcontent.com/pod-product-compliance
Lightning Source LLC
Chambersburg PA
CBHW071147260626
47162CB00003B/948